MW01094358

Carol's Christmas Awakening

LEYA LAYNE

I hope you
like your
Hallmark
Hot!

L Layne

Trigger Warnings

While this book is meant to be a quick and easy holiday read with a lot of spice, there are discussions of topics that could be triggering for readers. To be respectful to those who need warnings and those who see them as spoilers, I have placed the trigger warnings on my website. Scan this code to check the site.

This is a work of fiction. Names, characters, places, and incidents are products of the author's imagination or are used fictitiously and are not to be construed as real. Any resemblance to actual events, locals, organizations, or persons, living or dead, is entirely coincidental.

No portion of this book may be reproduced in any form without written permission from the publisher or author, except as permitted by U.S. copyright law.

Copyright © 2023 B. Isabel Writes
All rights reserved.
Ebook ISBN: 978-1-961045-03-3
Paperback ISBN-13: 978-1-961045-04-0

Dedicated to every woman over 40 who wonders whether their dreams for life and love are even worth pursuing. Finding love, enjoying life, pursuing dreams...none of these things is exclusively for the young.

I also have to thank my writing groups. I would not have gotten this book done on time without them. A huge motivator in this indie author journey is knowing we're not alone.

Chapter One

CAROL

As soon as the bell chimed, Clarissa's voice penetrated the shop.

"Ooh wee, that's a lot of Christmas candy outside."

I smiled at her exuberance and then shook my head to clear the emotion from my face. I loved the girl, but I would not encourage her lustful machinations. Not that Clarissa needed any encouragement in that area. She should have been called the Pied Piper of Ardor Point for the guys who followed her around like puppies.

"They've been outside making a racket since 7:45." I made sure my voice carried through the shop over the din of construction outside. The arrival of the Christmas Tree pop-up shop to the lot always caused a commotion, literally and figuratively. Regardless, they drummed up a lot of extra business each year, which was much appreciated.

"So, you know what time they got here, huh? You haven't been peeking, have you?" Clarissa's blonde hair bounced from behind the aisle before she came around the cooler carrying an armful of pink and yellow tea roses and a handful of baby's breath. She was dressed in her traditional goth attire, complete with thick eyeliner and black lips. The style was less a matter of lifestyle interest and more of a habit since Clarissa's high school, stick-it-to-mom days. Her fishnet stockings had pink ribbons laced through them that ended in an adorable bow right below the hem of her miniskirt, her long legs drawing the eye up.

"Mrs. Jensen will be here in 30 minutes for that bouquet."

"I know," Clarissa said with a smirk. "That's why I grabbed the flowers on my way back. It wasn't because I felt the need for thorn pricks this morning." She cocked her head in the direction of the outside noise. "I might be convinced to consider another type of prick, though."

"You're incorrigible, Rissa."

Clarissa winked and turned to the prep counter. I smiled and went back to the casket spray I had been working on before she arrived. Our town had grown significantly in recent years, but it was still small enough that I knew everyone. I handled every funeral request personally, and today's job was no different, though it felt different. I had just gotten word the town had experienced another loss that took me by surprise.

Mr. Moore had been such a sweet person. Even at 85, he would walk into the shop every week and buy a bouquet of hydrangeas for his wife of 60 years. They somehow managed to find the love story romance novels promised. Thinking about Mrs. Moore and how she'd never get flowers again, provoked tears that fell onto the arrangement.

"Do you need me to do this one for you?" Clarissa put her hand on my shoulder.

"No. I'll be fine. This one is easy. I didn't know him as well. I just got caught up thinking about Mr. Moore and how won't be coming in here Saturday mornings anymore. It's the end of an era, the end of a love story."

She gave me a sad smile. "You know, you're awfully sentimental for someone who has sworn off men and the possibility of love."

"The odds aren't in our favor. I'm tired of placing bets and losing. The Moores beat the house." My smile shone through the tears.

"Maybe. But sometimes the game itself is the reward." Clarissa said, and I shook my head, hoping she'd leave the conversation right there. "You wouldn't be crying on the petals if you had something else to occupy your mind and fill that emptiness." Clarissa leaned back and gestured widely at her lower midsection while gyrating her hips. The movement was so cartoonish and vulgar that I couldn't help but laugh. "You know I'm right."

"You are not right in the head, and I don't pay you to analyze my sex life."

The bell on the door chimed again. We both looked up before Clarissa whispered, "That would require you to have one."

I stepped into the workroom room to fix my face and left Clarissa to greet the customers. Immediate regret set in the moment I walked back out to the counter and heard Clarissa's flirtatious laugh.

"Carol will be out in a second. She needed to grab some things from the back. We're always glad to have extra hands around during the holidays."

"Nick, so good to see you again." I moved into the aisle nearest the door and greeted the old man with a quick a hug. "How have you been, Santa?"

Nick's eyes sparkled beneath his thick white brows when he smiled. Though his beard was trimmed short, he resembled Santa Claus more each year. His thick mountain accent spread warmth through the shop. "Carol, you're a sight for sore eyes. I bet ya done got married on me, didn't ya?"

"Not a chance. You know I'm waiting for you to retire and

come down off that mountain for good." I really did like the old man and worried about him up there in the winter.

"Them mountains been good to me."

I looked over at Clarissa who hadn't gone back to the bouquet she'd been working on. Instead, she was batting her lashes at the others hovering behind Nick. I cleared my throat and laughed when Clarissa jumped. With a raised eyebrow, I tipped my head toward the back of the shop.

"Mrs. Jensen's bouquet. I'm on it," Clarissa said, as she sauntered down the aisle. Sauntered was the only way to describe her slow, swaying walk toward the counter. A quick look over the group of four young men said that they had noticed the show as well. I rolled my eyes before turning my attention fully back to Nick.

"Looks like you brought some friends with you, Nick. Lots of new faces this year." Each of the men standing behind him looked young, maybe mid-twenties. It wasn't like Nick to leave a group of young ones on their own down here. "Are you hanging around for the season?"

"Nah, I got too much going on at the farm. Let me introduce this year's team." He proceeded to give me their names, and though I shook each man's hand, the details were a blur. There was a tall, lanky blond and a short, muscular young man who might have been indigenous with his dark hair and strong cheekbones. One of the other men was named Peter and another Travis, but I couldn't keep the four of them straight. I was too busy trying to figure out who was going to be in charge because I did not want the responsibility of managing the shop and Nick's employees too.

The door chimed, and Nick stuck his head out the door to yell. "Jackson, bring yourself in here for a second, boy. I need ya."

Please tell me this is not another kid, I thought while trying to catch a glimpse of this Jackson through the glass door. The person who approached the door from between the rows of wrapped trees was no kid. He wasn't overly tall, maybe five-eleven, but his broad shoulders and strong arms that barely fit inside the grey henley he wore said that he was all man. If that wasn't enough the salt sprinkled through his dark beard brought him fully into the grown ass man category. My cheeks flushed when he entered the shop and looked my way.

"Carol, this is my grandson, Jackson."

It took a moment to process Nick's statement before I could take the hand Jackson offered. "Your grandson?"

"Yeah," Nick said with a sheepish grin. "He's going to be taking over the business when I retire, so he's here from California for the season to start learning the ropes. He'll be foreman for this group of youngins and keep them out of your hair."

"It's not my hair I'm worried about them getting into," I said under my breath with an emphasis on the 'my'. Jackson, who was still standing far too close, chuckled. Shit, he'd heard that. *Don't look up. Don't look up, Carol.* I couldn't help it. He was staring, and heat rose up my neck. I was about to clarify that I'd meant Clarissa when Nick corralled the team out the door and said his farewells. Jackson was still smiling when he turned to leave.

I stood there, watching them through the window, focused entirely on Jackson's tight jeans. I was so distracted that I jumped when the door chimed again.

"Dammit!"

"Have I come at a bad time, Carol?" Mrs. Jensen's soft voice triggered another round of flushed skin.

"No, of course not. The bell scared me is all. My apologies. Clarissa should have your bouquet ready at the counter."

"I see old man Nick is setting up them trees. I think he comes earlier each year."

They were a week earlier than normal, but I wasn't going to feed into her fishing expedition. "He always opens the weekend before Thanksgiving." I gave her a patient smile that had been honed over the past decade of living in this small town. It was the only way to handle gossip.

"He's got a new crew with him. Hopefully, them boys can contain themselves around the young ladies in town. You know what happens when the youth get bored."

"They are all adults, and they have a foreman responsible for ensuring the work gets done. That is all I'm concerned about."

Mrs. Jensen turned away in a huff and made her way toward the back of the shop. If she didn't come back through in five minutes, I would go back there and save Clarissa from her benevolent warnings. Little did Mrs. Jensen know that those young men were in more danger of falling for Clarissa's charms than she was of falling for theirs. Laughing at my own joke, I looked back out the window before heading toward the counter. There was no one of interest left out there.

Clarissa turned on me as soon as the chimes announced Mrs. Jensen's departure. "So, who was the hottie with the beard?"

"He's too old for you, young lady," I retorted with a sarcastic smile and went back to finishing the arrangement I'd left sitting when Nick had entered the shop.

"What was that song from your generation? Age ain't nuthin but a number."

Normally, I would ignore Clarissa's bursts of random interest in the men who entered the shop. Though we regularly bantered like sisters, this time, my heart rate was rising, and my ears were tingling like my body was preparing for a fight. Focusing on the flowers in my hand, I tried to control my breathing, but Clarissa was watching, waiting for a response.

"Smart ass."

"Really? That's the best you could do?" Clarissa clicked her teeth and walked toward the front of the store, broom in hand.

I was just as disappointed in myself at that response. It was lame as hell. What was worse is I had no idea why I'd gotten so defensive at the simple question. Jackson was a hottie. Just because I was a self-imposed spinster didn't mean I was blind. "Nick must've been a looker when he was younger," I muttered to myself and set to finishing the spray.

With the floral arrangement carefully placed in its box and labeled with the funeral parlor's address, I carried it into the back room to place in the large cooler until tomorrow. I'd deliver it tomorrow morning, so the flowers would be fresh for the viewing and the funeral. No sooner had I passed through the swinging saloon-style doors that the front door chimed again.

"Clarissa!"

"I'm on it," came the girl's voice from the opposite end of the shop.

Less than a minute later, Clarissa was standing in the doorway with a sly grin. "I'm going to take my lunch. Are you good?" I raised an eyebrow, but Clarissa just smirked and turned on her heel.

She came back in the shop after lunch in a flurry of expletives. "Holy shit! Can you believe that old man?" I barely had a second to look up from the arrangement I was creating before she continued her tirade. "Nick left these guys down here and didn't even tell them where they could eat or even what hotel the team normally stayed at. He just expected them to figure it out on their own."

"Whoa, slow down," I said, waving my hand for her to catch her breath.

The news was a bit shocking. Nick usually did a great job

taking care of his guys. He'd get them set up before he'd head back up the mountain, and then he'd come down every week or so to check in with them. If he already left this crew floundering on day one, what would things be like for them in the coming weeks? Clarissa didn't give me a chance to delve more deeply into that thought, as she barreled through the rest of her story.

"Anyway, I got three and a possible on those younger guys. Though that Jackson is a hottie, I think you're right about him being too old for me, or rather too serious. Serious is boring," she said with a flourish, knocking her hip against mine before disappearing into the back room.

My mouth stood wide open. I hadn't even been able to get one word in on the conversation. Three and a possible? I didn't even want to think about that one. And what did Clarissa mean about serious and boring. I'm not boring, I thought to myself. *Am I?*

Chapter Two

CAROL

The next few days passed in a blur. Customers came and left. Some even bought flowers. Most, however, used the flower shop as an excuse to look at the new guys. No use getting upset. The same thing happened every year when the trees arrived. Such is life in a small town.

I was in the back putting finishing touches on the deliveries for the morning when the door chimed unexpectedly. Clarissa had already left for the day, and, technically, the shop was closed. She must have forgotten to lock the door on her way out. Turning around, I came face-to-face with Jackson, who was standing in the doorway of the workroom.

"Oh," I exclaimed, dropping the flowers in my hands.

He stepped into the room and squatted to retrieve the half dozen long-stemmed Osiris roses, picking up the white and red petals that came loose when the flowers hit the floor. "I'm sorry. I didn't mean to startle you." He handed me the stems. He was so close, I could smell the cool outdoor air on him mixed with a faded cologne I couldn't quite place. Still, he smelled as good as he looked.

"You're fine. I heard the door chime but didn't expect anyone to be this close already. We're technically closed." Recognizing the start of nervous rambling, I caught myself and shifted the subject. "How can I help you?"

"I wanted to come by and thank you for letting Clarissa show us around during lunches this week."

I put up a hand to stop him. "Let's get one thing straight. I don't let Clarissa do anything. That girl has a mind of her own, and I'm not sure she would listen to me if I told her not to do something."

He chuckled, and my knees softened. He was far too close and far too fine. Sweat began to trickle down the back of my neck.

"I gathered that from spending an hour with her and my team each day, but I wanted to come by and say thanks anyway. I hate to admit that I was not fully prepared for this adventure, nor did I expect my grandfather to leave so quickly after we arrived. I'm usually a planner." He gave her a sheepish grin that was very similar to Nick's.

"Well, in Nick's defense, I'm sure he's used to his team knowing where to go and where things are." This was the first year in the partnership where the whole team had been brand new. Jackson's demeanor changed. He looked down at the floor, and his expression was forlorn. There was a story behind that look, and I almost asked him about it. Needless to say, I didn't finish my last thoughts aloud.

He quickly recovered, put a smile back on his face, and looked deep into my eyes. He was still standing close enough to touch. I was taken aback at how much I wanted to do just that. My fingertips were itching to see if his skin would be warm or if it held the coolness of the foothills in November. What was it about him? I took a step back and broke the spell.

"So, that's all I wanted to do was say thank you," he said

far too quickly. He turned to leave but immediately returned with a business card in his hand. "Oh, and to give you this. Here is my cell number and my room at the hotel. If you need anything, or if something happens here while I'm gone, please don't hesitate to give me a call or come find me. Have a good night." This time, when he turned away, he did leave the shop.

I took a deep, shuddering breath. He unnerved me in a way I hadn't felt in years. "Get yourself together, girl," I said aloud as I went to lock the front door. The men climbed into the two trucks they'd arrived with. I looked at the business card in my hand and shook my head. He didn't have to say which hotel they were at. Nick's team always stayed at the same hotel. I wouldn't tell him that, though. In fact, I planned to avoid him for the next month if at all possible.

I finished the dinner I'd grabbed on my way home. It wasn't that I didn't know how to cook. It was more that I hated cooking just for myself. Actually, it wasn't the cooking. It was the amount of work it took to prep, cook, and clean up that I hated. If anyone asked, I'd tell them my home was a sanctuary, but there were some things that sucked about living alone. Chores were one of them.

After throwing away the to-go tray, I headed toward my bedroom. It had been an interesting day, so, of course, my thoughts turned to the stranger whose presence had oddly knocked me off-kilter. Not only was he fine, he was different from all the men in the area. His walk was different, and his voice was different. He had an air about him that said quiet sophistication. Yet, he played the lumberjack very well. I shook my head. *We are not going there.*

My cat, Miel, responded to my verbal musings with a

chirp. "I wasn't talking to you, girl." I scratched the honey-colored cat on her head. "I'm going to take a shower and prepare myself to start all over again tomorrow." I quickly looked around the empty room in case someone heard me talking to my cat and laughed. There was a better chance of a hot shower washing away thoughts of Jackson than someone else being in the house listening to me slowly meld into a crazy cat lady.

The hot water running over my back gradually loosened my tense muscles. Showers were the best when the water made my skin tingle with licks of fire all over. It quickly relaxed me, allowing me to focus on washing my hair. Long gone were the days where I had to gather my tresses on top of my head just to work the shampoo in. Now, in my mid-forties, I didn't want that daily hassle, so I kept my hair short. Often, like this evening, my hands went on autopilot and poured more shampoo than was needed.

Suds ran over my body, caressing the curves of my neck and sliding down my shoulders and between my breasts. I leaned back into the water spray and closed my eyes. As the bubbles raced from my hair and through my fingers, I conjured an image of Jackson. He was standing in the doorway of the workshop, just inches from me. Though I had been able to contain myself in the shop, the combination of heat from the water, silky suds caressing my skin, and the deepening heat in my core, fueled my imagination.

In my mind, I reached out and grabbed his shirt, pulling him to me. He opened his mouth in surprise, and I locked onto his open lips, teasing them with my tongue and nibbling them with my teeth. His hands slid from my hips to my waist, and he pulled me against him. My hands followed the trails of water down across my already puckered nipples, and I gave them a little pinch. I could hear my own ragged breaths, but I couldn't stop. I was caught between two sets of hands, one a daydream and the other my own.

I gave in to the sensations and held his hands in place on my hips while I turned around until my ass was pressed firmly against the hard promise held in his taut jeans. I leaned against the shower wall, my hands finding the space between my thick thighs. My muscles tensed when fingers brushed against my labia. I pictured Jackson following my silent instruction to slide his hand into my waistband. I undid the button and zipper to give him better access. When a hand firmly grasped my fat lips, I gasped, and when a finger slipped between them, the tip tickling my clit, I slid to the floor of the shower.

I lay there panting long after the pulsing of my release subsided. It had been years since I allowed myself a moment of lustful weakness. The intentional decision to abstain from sex was necessary to keep me from repeating the errors of my last lust-driven shituationship. I had thought the relationship had developed into something more, but I'd been dead wrong. I barely made it out alive. I'd gladly sworn off sex and men and had lived the past ten years as a spinster florist, never questioning that decision until today. I would definitely need to stay as far away from Jackson as possible if I was going to get myself back in check.

"Fuck!" I slammed my palms against the floor of the shower and stood. When I turned off the water that had already gone tepid, Miel was scratching at the bathroom door. Wrapping a towel around myself, I rolled my eyes at the current state of my life. "Yep, sign me up for the crazy cat lady awards." I opened the bathroom door, and Miel turned back toward the kitchen. I sighed at her indifference.

Chapter Three
CAROL

I woke in a pissy mood still frustrated with my unwanted response to the new guy in town. I thought about taking the day off, but I hated leaving Clarissa to run the shop all day once the season started. There were also some important deliveries to make, not the least of which was to the funeral home. That thought got me moving.

The temperature was much cooler this morning than it had been yesterday, and my car was a bit sluggish to start. I talked to it soothingly and chalked its discontent up to a combination of my own mood and the weather. I'd spend all season blaming any number of things on the weather. Truth be told, I hated the cold, but I liked it here in this little town at the foot of the Appalachian Mountains.

I arrived at the shop before anyone, so I had time to set up the cash box, prioritize the floral arrangements we needed to make for the day, and begin packing the deliveries in the car. Being the first one in also meant that I would likely avoid seeing Jackson. If Clarissa got here early enough, I could potentially leave before the men came to open the tree shop that now took over half the parking lot. Of course, I wasn't that lucky. Clarissa strolled in exactly on time, and noise already radiated from the tents outside.

"I don't remember them ever starting this early last year," Clarissa said with a huge yawn she quickly covered with a sip of her equally large takeout coffee.

"I was just thinking the same thing. Long night?" The girl smiled but said nothing. I eyed her suspiciously. "You don't ever stay quiet about your nighttime exploits. So, which of the three and a possible was it?"

Clarissa snorted. "That possible was a little too easy," she said with a huge grin.

I couldn't help but laugh at her. She reminded me so much of myself when I was younger. I used to be bold and open too. Hopefully, Rissa would never have an experience break her confidence. Though I worried about her, I loved watching her run the world.

"How many deliveries do you have today?"

Before Clarissa could read my thoughts, I looked down at the list in my hands, though I had already memorized the order. "Seven. I'm not gonna lie, every day I'm surprised at how well business is going. I was really nervous when I first opened this shop here in town."

"You're good to people, Carol. You care about them, and they know it. You keep your prices down, and you try to integrate yourself into the town, unlike most transplants up here. You didn't try to change it to suit you."

"I think that's the nicest thing you've ever said to me," I responded, my smile dripping sarcasm.

"Yeah, well, there's only enough room in here for one bitch per day." We both laughed, as the door chimed with the first customer of the morning.

"You handle that, and I'll be back after I make these deliveries." I reached for my keys and jacket. "I already left the list of arrangements we need to make today on the counter in the back."

"I'm on it," Carissa responded, heading toward the customer without missing a beat.

I was proud of the mirror placements around the shop that let us see customer movements throughout the labyrinth of flowers and decorative arrangements. Not only was it great for safety, but it also allowed us to provide quick service no matter where customers stood. I smiled to myself and headed for the door.

None of the men were visible outside, probably because there were so many trees standing around the perimeter of the tent. I quickly got into my car and turned the key. Nothing. I tried it again. Nothing, not a whir or a click. Nothing happened. "Shit," I yelled and slapped the steering wheel. "I thought we had an agreement, you and I," I said to the car, slamming the door before opening the hood.

I almost felt his presence before I heard his voice. It was an odd realization and one that did not help my mood any. "Do you need some help," he asked casually. I steeled myself.

"No, I'm fine. I think my battery might be dead. It was making funny noises this morning when I left the house, but I thought maybe it was just responding to the early morning coolness." I didn't mention thinking the car was potentially responding to my own mood. If he asked why I was in a bad mood, I wasn't sure I could stop myself from telling him it was because I imagined his hands all over me last night. That statement would not get him to stay in the tent and away from me. Now, with him standing this close, I wasn't even sure if that was the response I wanted from him anyway.

"Let me go bring the truck over and see if we can't give her a jump," he said and stepped away, oblivious of my inner turmoil. I relaxed a little, when I heard his footsteps on the gravel.

Clarissa popped her head out of the shop. "Everything all right?"

"Stupid car won't start. Jackson is going to try to jump it with the truck."

"Guess he can be good for something, huh?"

I gave her a scathing look, as Jackson pulled the truck up to the car's bumper, blocking my view of the shop door. We tried starting the car three different times, and it just would not turn over. "Shit! I don't have time for this."

"Is there anything I can do," Jackson asked with a genuine look of concern.

"No, I just have to make these deliveries. One of them is to the funeral home for this afternoon's memorial. I hate to disappoint Mrs. Moore." I looked toward the back seat, and unwanted tears burned my eyes. Without a word, Jackson walked around the car and opened the back door. "What are you doing?" He didn't answer right away. I ran around the other side to find him gathering packages into his arms. "Jackson, what do you think you're doing?"

"Look, our businesses have a partnership, which means, we both must be able to do our jobs. I'm going to help you with yours today." He walked toward his truck with the deliveries and deposited them on the back seat. When he came back toward me with a determined look, my breath hitched, and my mind flashed back to last night's daydream. I stared into his face, my heart beating in rhythm to his footfalls.

At the last moment, he sidestepped me and reached back into the car for the other packages. "Are there more than this," he asked. His voice was muffled from leaning inside the vehicle, and it took a few seconds for my mind to register what was happening. "Carol? Are you ok?"

"What? Yes. No, there aren't any others. You know you don't have to do this, right? I'll call AAA and get a new battery."

He looked skeptical. "They have AAA here?"

That broke my stupor and made me laugh, a full belly laugh. "Of course, they do. What kind of question is that? Ardor Point isn't backwoods."

"Either way, I'm here, we're not exactly busy, and it gives me a chance to learn this 'not backwoods' town better. Humor me."

He held out his hand and led me to the passenger side, helping me climb into the seat. This day was definitely not going the way I had hoped. Not only did I have to see and talk with him, but now I would be spending the better part of the morning sitting next to him. Fuck, he smelled good.

Chapter Four
JACKSON

We traveled in relative silence through the first few deliveries, other than her giving me directions. I wasn't sure if she was just having a bad day in general or disliked me specifically. In her workroom yesterday, I saw something like a flash of interest in her eyes when we were close, but she covered it up so quickly, maybe I had imagined it. I left before common sense disappeared and I acted on the desire to ignite that spark. She was so serious and wound so tightly, I wanted to unwrap her and find her soft middle. No doubt there was one. Her conservative dress and sensible shoes didn't match the cool demeanor that was better suited for the boardroom than a flower shop. She was intriguing.

I watched her from the corner of my eye. Her hands were clasped in her lap, and her legs pressed tightly together. Her long skirt and sweater did nothing to hide her thick thighs and ample bosom when everything pulled tight from the way she had climbed into the truck. I wiped my right hand on my jeans. My palm itched to sit on her thigh. She was watching my hand, and a wave of desire surged straight to my groin. If I didn't get my thoughts in order, she'd be watching me readjust myself.

"Would you like to stop for a cup of coffee," I asked to shift attention away from those rogue ideas.

"I don't like coffee."

"Seriously?"

"Please don't start with the 'how do you not like coffee' and 'coffee is life' crap, ok."

"You don't have to worry about that with me. I don't like it either. I'm just not used to finding someone else who doesn't. In Cali, most people would like to hook up a coffee IV in one hand and hold a beer in the other."

"It's not just in California," she said between laughing breaths. I liked her laugh. It was light and breathy. She was a walking contradiction, and it drew me in. Would her moans be that bright or would she hide them like she does her body? I tried to control my wayward thoughts with an admonishing *Whoa, big guy!* As soon the words left my mouth, I regretted them. I squeezed my eyes shut hoping she hadn't heard but knowing my luck wasn't that good.

"I'm sorry," she said with a lilt that definitely expressed a question.

Dammit. Her eyes were fixed on my face, and I was sure she'd see my embarrassment written there. I looked out the driver's side window trying to think of something to say. I hadn't meant to say that aloud.

"So, beer is out too then?"

She laughed again and turned her body toward me, knee brought up on the seat, her skirt the only thing hiding a glorious view. I somehow managed to pull my gaze quickly up to her face before she read my thoughts as loudly as if I'd spoken them...again. When we came to a stoplight, I turned toward her fully. She had one eyebrow cocked.

"Nice try," she said. "That's not what you said. I'm still not sure what exactly it was, but it did not sound like 'so beer is out too then.'" She mocked me, deepening her voice. I couldn't help but laugh.

"That is not how I sound."

"It is when you're trying to bullshit."

My eyebrows raised at that. "Oh really. Well, what if I was saying that you have a beautiful laugh that doesn't quite match how you present yourself?"

She looked down and turned away. I could've punched myself. "Hey, I apologize if I said something offensive. I was enjoying the banter after nearly an hour of silence."

"I'm not offended, and I understand. I'm not always the best company."

Little did she realize, her company was a breath of fresh air. I'd come out here to get away from the stress and stuffiness of my California life. I wanted to clear my head and maybe relive some of those childhood memories I'd remembered fondly. My grandfather didn't exactly offer a warm welcome, and then he sent me here off the mountain under the pretense of preparing me to take over the business. The team was cool and all, but they were young and unfocused. I didn't have much in common with them. She, on the other hand, shone like a beacon of quiet stability from the moment we were introduced.

"The funeral parlor is up ahead on the right," she said, breaking the silence.

She gave such a withered look when I offered to help her carry the flowers into the funeral parlor that I didn't bother getting out of the truck. I was still kicking myself for the way the conversation turned when it had been flowing so well. *Way to go, dumbass.* Why couldn't I have just said something innocuous like 'thinking aloud,' or some other such ridiculous thing. I knew how to bullshit with the best of them, and what I didn't know already, Diane had taught me. Carol was

LEYA LAYNE

nothing like Diane, though, which was a good thing. Still, what was it about Carol that made me hope she'd jump at the chance to one-up me until we were both left breathless? There was nothing in her demeanor that said I'd be successful, nothing except that occasional flash in her eyes. My dumb ass was about to get my balls handed to me over some wishful thinking.

As I sat waiting, my thoughts turned to the team. Had they had any customers? By my calculation, Nick had us set up shop at least two weeks too early. Did he open every year at this time, or was this year special because I was here? I already knew this novice team of young guys was purposeful. The old man probably sent them here to languish in boredom just to see if I could hold them together. I just wasn't sure if it was a punishment or a test. Either way, I was determined to make it a successful endeavor, if for nothing else to spite him.

Though I wouldn't have admitted how diligently I'd watched the door, I saw the moment Carol exited the back of the building. She must not have realized I was watching because she stopped outside the door and leaned against the wall, wiping at her face. Was she crying? I sat there frozen, torn between wanting to check on her and knowing she'd reject the concern. When her shoulders shuddered in sobs, the decision was made. Ten paces, and I wrapped my arms around her shoulders, pulling her in close.

Chapter Five

CAROL

Every time I've made one of these deliveries, I've barely been able to hold in the tears. This one just hit a little harder. It was like I knew them. I'd watched their love story with awe and wonder. Mr. Moore's obvious adoration for his wife kept me from being completely jaded against the idea of love. It could happen and work, even if it wasn't in the cards for me. I hugged Mrs. Moore before exiting the funeral parlor and barely made it outside when the sobs took over.

In one moment, I was hyperventilating, and the next, I was wrapped in Jackson's arms. *Where had he come from?* I hadn't heard his approach, but I quickly wrapped my arms around his waist and leaned in. We stood like that for what felt like forever. He held me tight and rubbed my hair. I breathed in his scent until my breath steadied. When I pulled away, I had to quickly wipe at his chest where his shirt was soaked. Hopefully, it was just tears. The thought made me giggle before I brought myself to look up into his face. His sympathetic eyes were almost enough to make me reach up and kiss him.

He smiled down at me, holding my shoulder with one arm and brushing a rogue hair from my face with the other hand. I couldn't help it. I reached a hand up and cupped his cheek. "Thank you," I whispered. His eyes shifted from compassion to desire a moment before he captured my open lips with his own. I froze for just a second before giving in to my own desire. I moved my hand to the back of his neck, pulling him in tighter. He reached down and grabbed my ass with both hands, a growl slipping from his throat as our tongues danced.

He released my lips, and I involuntarily whimpered. Then he trailed his lips down to my neck, producing a sigh. He ran his tongue from the crease of my neck up to my ear lobe, making me tremble. "It's a good thing you are so well-covered, else I'd have already buried my face between your thighs. As it is, I think we should probably leave before everyone gets a show."

"That's very sensible of you, thanks." Of course, he was right, but I wasn't ready to lose his warmth. I turned my face into his neck and pulled the skin between my teeth. He hissed, and his fingers dug into my ass, as he nearly lifted me from the ground. I was ready to have him make good on that last threat when my phone rang. "Dammit!" It was the shop's ringtone. Giving him an apologetic smile, I pulled away to answer it. As we walked toward the truck, I noticed him stagger, readjusting his jeans, and I smiled.

Chapter Six

CAROL

We had barely arrived back at the shop when one of Jackson's guys, Travis, if I remembered right, and Clarissa both came running toward the truck from opposite sides.

"Boss, the cops were here," Travis blurted before Jackson could get his door fully opened.

"You are never going to believe what happened," Clarissa said as she yanked open my door.

Jackson and I exchanged glances and both headed to our respective shops. I walked into a building bustling with customers, most of which seemed to be watching out the windows more than looking at the flowers. Jackson and Travis walked toward the tents, weaving between the groups of people who were standing around outside. They were likely pretending to look at the trees as much as our visitors were pretending to be interested in the fern selection.

I addressed each person by name, garnering embarrassed

smiles from most. Those people filed out of the building after returning a curt greeting. The shop was soon empty, except for two actual customers there to peruse the new mums that had just arrived for Thanksgiving. Clarissa and I set to work securing their purchases. When those final customers were gone, I locked the door.

"What in the hell happened here?"

"You will never believe it!"

"You said that already." I tapped my foot, turning away from the view out the front door to Clarissa.

"No sooner had we gotten off the phone than the cops showed up. In true Ardor Point fashion, the town arrived minutes later."

"Showed up here, at the shop?"

"No! They came looking for Freddy."

"Who is Freddy?"

Clarissa rolled her eyes in a way that said I should know who Freddy was. Thankfully, the girl didn't wait to answer the question anyway, as it was part of her excited story. "Freddy is the tall, lanky blond that works in the tents."

"One of the foresters?"

"Yeah, apparently, he went out to lunch and accosted one of the servers behind the diner."

"What?"

"That's what Marc said the cops told him when they came looking for Freddy. They said Amy from the diner called 911 because one of her girls returned from taking out the trash all tore up. She said he'd followed her outside. I don't know the details because we got interrupted by the throng of nosy neighbors who flooded both shops."

"Oh no!" I walked to the back and sat on one of the stools we kept behind the counter. I had been worried about the new team, but I'd never have expected anything like this. None of them had looked predatory. Of course, David hadn't been a predator either until he was. I shuddered, as memories flooded. "That poor girl. Is she ok?"

"The cops said she was just shaken up a bit from where he had grabbed her. She had mace in her pocket, thankfully. They said she sprayed him and then ran back inside. He was gone by the time Amy and the cook went to look for him."

I couldn't stop shaking. I had invited strangers into the town. I didn't vet them, but I trusted Nick. If I hadn't allowed Jackson to drive me around, maybe he would have been there to better supervise the comings and goings of his team.

"Carol, are you ok?"

I shook my head against the memories and growing panic. "What? Oh, yeah, I'm good. Just wondering what we could've done to prevent this."

"Nothing. You could have done nothing. That's not how it works, and there's no point in working yourself up about it. Dude had issues, and I'm so glad I wasn't feeling his vibe the more time I spent with him. Anyway, the team is worried about Jackson and what will happen when Nick finds out."

"What do you mean?"

"According to Marc, he was the original possible I hooked up with, the old man specifically drove into the city to find guys to work this team. He chose dudes he didn't know who had never worked at a tree farm or ran a tree shop before. It was all a quick turnaround. They had to be ready to head up the mountain the following morning and were shown the types of trees they'd be selling. That was it. Within a week, they loaded up the trucks, were introduced to Jackson as their foreman for the season, and dropped here without so much as a good luck."

I sat there slack-jawed. Nothing I knew of the old man I'd been working with for the last five holiday seasons reconciled with the situation this year. I knew something was strange when no one from previous years had come with the team, but to think this was all intentional. My anger rose. He had sent

Jackson here to fail and sent a predator to my doorstep. I jumped off the stool and was looking for my phone when someone knocked on the door.

"I'll see who it is," Clarissa offered.

"Tell them we're closed for the remainder of the day."

"I'm on it."

I watched my assistant walk around the aisles toward the door and then tracked the girl using the mirror system. I was feeling extra protective at the moment and wished I could see out the doorway. I'd have to readjust those mirrors. Within seconds, Clarissa was heading back, though I hadn't heard the door latch. I met her halfway.

"Jackson is at the door asking to speak with you. He seems worried about you." When I didn't immediately respond, Clarissa looked at me more intently. I tried to maintain a sense of aloofness but must have failed miserably. "Something happened between the two of you while making deliveries." It wasn't a question.

"Nothing happened," I lied. "He caught me crying outside of the funeral parlor, as I always do, and he comforted me." Clarissa's eyebrow raised. The girl was way too perceptive. "Invite him in and then give us a minute, ok." Clarissa smiled a knowing smile and walked away.

The look on Jackson's face was one of controlled fury. He'd obviously heard the story from his men. "I do not like the idea that I will be coming here to offer you an apology for one thing or another every evening," he said, his voice barely a whisper.

"What do you need to apologize for?"

"The behavior of my team reflects on me, and the fact that we are in your parking lot, partnering with you, reflects on you. If I knew where that kid was right now, I'd beat the shit out of him and haul his ass to the police myself, but since he hasn't returned, all I can do is offer you an apology."

"His behavior wasn't your fault. Clarissa just had to

remind me of that because I sat here beating myself up for a moment as well."

He stared at me, his mouth opening like he wanted to say something, but I held up a hand to stop him. "Why did Nick send you here with this team?" The way he deflated at that question had me wanting to apologize, but I also wanted an answer.

"I don't really know, honestly." I nearly scoffed, but the truth was written in his eyes. "I sat in the truck this afternoon wondering that same thing. Perhaps it's a test to see if I am worthy of being his heir, or maybe he's punishing me for something."

"Punishing you?"

"I don't know, but it damn sure feels like a punishment. May I," he asked, indicating the stool behind the counter. I nodded, and he took a seat, shoulders slumping in. "I told the guys to close up for the day. No one standing around was actually trying to buy anything anyway."

"I told Clarissa the same thing. That's why the door was locked. Wanna go get a drink? You look like you need one." He smiled, and his eyes lit up. He was truly an attractive man. Even his vulnerability was a turn on. "You'll have to drive though, as I haven't had a chance to get a new battery for my car."

"No worries. Let me get those guys to the hotel, and I'll come back for you."

He left without another word, probably so I couldn't change my mind. I probably should have changed my mind after our moment outside the funeral parlor.

Clarissa walked in and asked if she needed to help close up. The smirk on her face said she still did not believe nothing was happening between Jackson and me, but I refused to feed into her curiosity. I wouldn't have known what to say even if I wanted to.

From behind us, the door opened, and Marc popped his

head in. "Clarissa, are you leaving soon, or do you just want to meet me later?"

Clarissa smiled and winked before turning to leave.

"Don't do anything I wouldn't do," I yelled at her back.

"I plan to do everything you wouldn't," came Clarissa's voice before the door latched tight, and the lock turned into place.

I had no doubt that she meant just that, but it didn't settle my worry for her every time she left each night. It also didn't calm my anxiety about what would happen the next time Jackson and I were alone. Men weren't on the agenda. I had sworn off them a decade ago, so to just fall into his arms, grief or not, was messing with my head.

Was he attractive? God, yes! Was he super sweet for offering to drive me all over town this morning? Yes. Was there something vulnerable in his apologies that tugged on my heart? Sure. Was that enough reason to jump his bones? No. So what the fuck was going on, and what was I going to do about it? I had no fucking idea.

I watched Jackson walk back into the tent after Clarissa and Marc pulled off and knew I didn't have much time to get things in order before he'd be knocking on the door again. I quickly made a to-do list for the morning, made sure all the fresh cuts were in water and the deliveries were organized. Then I took a deep breath, locked the shop door, and walked out the door over to the tent before I changed my mind about going for that drink.

Chapter Seven
JACKSON

I watched my guys jump into the other truck from inside the tent. Marc had decided to go out with Clarissa. He seemed really taken by the girl, and I had to laugh because they made such a seemingly odd couple. She was the complete opposite of Marc, commanding attention everywhere she went. If people weren't looking at her dress, they were shocked by her speech. The girl held nothing back. Marc, on the other hand, was laid back and quiet, a wallflower. He was happy to be here and working, tried not to draw attention to himself, even with the customers, and liked things simple and tidy. He was aways picking up after the other guys. I smiled as the two of them climbed into Clarissa's Acura MDX. The girl had style and money.

When everyone was gone, I walked back to the middle of the tent and looked around. I had long since secured the cash-box, putting all the money into the thick, leather locked bag that would stay in my truck until the morning. We hadn't had many sales, so there was no need for a bank run, but I didn't like to leave anything valuable in the tent overnight. Why did I even care, I asked myself for the umpteenth time that day. My grandfather didn't seem to care, so why was I still being so diligent? Then I thought about the guys I had just sent back to the hotel. I planned to pay them for the rest of the day because it wasn't their fault the shop was closing early. I'd had some misgivings about Freddy, but thought they'd maybe work out over time. Now that I understood that intuition, I wished I'd have taken it more to heart.

No sooner had I started on the downward spiral of self-flagellation when the jingle of the shop door opening and closing pierced the silence. At least Carol didn't blame me for today. I was tired of being blamed for things I couldn't control. Diane had blamed me for everything that did or didn't happen in our lives, which brought me out here to the middle of nowhere in the first place. Now, it seemed, my grandfather was blaming me for something as well, but I had no clue what that something might be. I listened to Carol's shoes on the gravel approaching the tent and pushed all those negative thoughts from my mind. I turned on a smile and met her at the tent flaps.

"Are you ready," she asked. My smile turned into a genuine one at seeing her, and I set to closing the flaps and activating the motion detection alarms.

"I am so ready," I responded before grabbing her hand. She stiffened a little at the gesture but then relaxed on the way to the truck. She actually smiled when I opened her door.

We made our way to a small pub on the other side of town, closer to the interstate than the shop. The name was a little tongue in cheek. The sign above the door said The Grecian Urn, and there was a portrait of an urn with a centaur on it. Taped to the door was an advertisement for live music performed by Siren. I chuckled, but when Carol looked up, I shook my head and just held the door open. The lights inside were dim, but the place felt cozy. There were booths lined up against the front wall on either side of the door and tables filled the rest of the floor. To the rear left was a stage with a red curtain. A piano sat in front of the curtain. To the rear right was the bar area, which was the most lit part of the establishment.

"Do you come here often," I asked.

Carol shook her head. "No, but I've passed this place many times since I moved here and have always wanted to come."

The bartender yelled across the room for us to grab whichever table we wanted. I led the way to a booth in the far corner across from the bar.

"So, what brought you to Ardor Point?" I asked, looking at her intently.

"That sounds like a loaded question from someone who didn't expect to be here himself."

I shrugged. "That's a long story too, and I'd rather hear yours."

"Oh, you won't get out of it that easily. If I have to free my skeletons, you do too."

I tried to hold back a laugh, but my lips still tweaked up in a half smile. Lucky for me, the server, a beautiful woman wearing a toga, interrupted us.

"Oh shit, you all take this Grecian thing seriously."

The server smiled after stopping her automatic eye roll. "The owner thinks that we're competing with the big-name bars that encourage ogling the girls. Does anyone see any big-name bars around here in Ardor Point." We both laughed with her.

After we placed our orders, a scotch on the rocks for me and a Long Island for her, the server returned to the bar.

"So, you were telling me how you got here," I said with a wink.

She sat quietly for a few moments, and I could only imagine she was wondering how much she wanted to tell me.

There was no way for me to prove that I wasn't the type to hold her story against her, especially since it seemed like she didn't share her past with anyone. Who knew, though. Maybe she'd find a stranger safer. She shrugged, and my eyebrows lifted involuntarily. Damn, I need to be less expressive. I said that last part aloud for her benefit and earned the chuckle I was hoping for.

"I've moved around a lot," she said. "I've lived a lot of life and had a lot of experiences in my 45 years on this planet." She nearly laughed when my eyes bulged. "Yes, I am 45." I couldn't believe it and sat there mouth opening and closing like a guppy. She rolled her eyes and laughed at me.

"There's no way in hell. I mean, I believe you, but damn, woman."

Carol smiled and turned toward the bar to hide the blush that was rushing up her neck. I caught it, though, before the server returned with our drinks. She wasn't a teenage girl to be blushing at random compliments, but I hoped that meant she was having a similar reaction to me as I had to her.

"Earth to Carol," I said with a grin once the server walked away again.

I couldn't hide the smirk on my face at her startled reaction, and I had to fight the urge to pull her into my lap just to catch her off guard. Only problem was, I was afraid of putting her into a position she might need, or want, to escape. Instead, I schooled my expression and raised an eyebrow.

"You were talking about the ancient wisdom you'd gained in all your years of experience."

The booth we occupied had a bench that encircled the table, and I had somewhat closed the distance between us. My arm was perched on the back of the bench behind her head, and I was casually leaned back in my seat, at least I hoped it looked casual. I took a sip from my drink and watched her eyes flash hot. She reached out and playfully swatted at my chest that was now within arms' reach. The look on her face said that I was quicker than she'd have thought possible when I grabbed her wrist with my free hand.

"Don't tell me this beautiful flower has thorns," I said, as I brought her wrist to my mouth and kissed it.

Carol froze and then shuddered. Her pulse quickened under my fingers, and I recognized her strong urge to pull away and run. She was looking toward the exit while trying to keep her breathing under control when I kissed her wrist. My brain, unable to correlate her visceral response and her actions, short circuited, at least that's what I would tell myself in the morning. She pushed the table out a bit and climbed into my lap. Our drinks sloshed, but neither of us noticed. I gasped and then a groan escaped my throat.

The server's voice cut through the lust-filled haze. "Should I bring you all the check...or maybe some ice water?" My hands froze on her ass before smoothing her skirt back down. Her lips left my neck, as she straightened the hem of my shirt over my waistband.

"The check," I said, my voice clearly demonstrating annoyance at the interruption. As soon as the young woman swiped my credit card, we both downed our forgotten drinks and headed for the door. "Where to," I asked.

Chapter Eight

JACKSON

We pulled into the shop's parking lot, and I turned the truck off.

"I need to grab a couple of things from inside," Carol said, without looking my way. "Would you be able to give me a ride home? I'll call AAA in the morning to get that battery. If not, I can call an Uber."

"Hey." There was so much I wanted to say, but really, I just wanted her to look at me. It took an excruciatingly long time before she did so. "I'm not going to bite, Carol. I have no intention of hurting you. I thought you were as interested as I by the way the world seems to stop when we're alone together."

She had been sitting ramrod straight, but something shifted. Whether it was my words or something else, her cold exterior melted. She looked into my eyes. "I am" was all she said. Thankfully, her eyes were illuminated by the emergency lights set up around the tree tent. I could see the truth of her interest in them and smiled.

"I'm glad to hear that. So, what keeps happening to make you change your mind or regret something that hasn't even happened?" I held myself back from saying 'yet,' afraid she'd freeze up again, so I was unprepared to hear her add the word with a bite of her lip. "You are a damn beautiful woman, and every part of me wants a taste of you, but I am patient."

Her cryptic response of "no regrets" knocked me for even more of a loop, and my head tilted to the side. I had to look like a hound dog waiting for its next command. She chuckled and warmness filled my chest.

"I mean, I don't regret anything, and my body reacts every time you're near or I hear your voice. None of which makes any sense considering how long it has been." I watched her turn introspective and held my tongue. "This is going to sound crazy, but I didn't think she still knew what lust was or how to respond to it. It's a bit unnerving."

"She," I asked, not sure what she was saying, though hoping for a bone.

The longer we talked, the more visibly comfortable she became. With that comfort came a level of confidence and boldness I wasn't expecting. I damn near jumped out of my skin at her next words. "Yes, this purring kitten of mine that wants you to rub her."

Not waiting for her to turn cold again, I pulled her into my lap, putting her back against the door, so her legs stretched across to the seat she had occupied just moments earlier. When I captured her mouth, she purred audibly. I reached down for the hem of her skirt and pulled it upward to her thighs. She broke off from the kiss and trailed her lips up my jawline. I stiffened beneath her. When she ran her tongue up to my earlobe and lightly nipped it with her teeth, I hissed.

"Touch me, Jackson," she whispered in my ear, as my hand

slid between her legs. I ran my fingers between her thighs and felt the heat emanating from her. I nearly howled with absolute joy at this moment I'd been dreaming of since Nick introduced us. Did she have any idea how hard it had been to not pick her up on my shoulders every time I caught her alone? I rubbed her through her panties until they were dripping, and she was panting.

"More?" I asked. "Tell me what you want, Carol."

She looked at my mouth and ran her tongue over her lips. When her gaze finally reached my eyes, I could read her desire loud and clear. I still wanted to hear her words. Rather than say anything, she held my gaze and grabbed my hand, pulling it up to her lips. My balls tightened instinctively when she opened her mouth and took my fingers into it. With her other hand, she grabbed my neck and pulled me close.

"I want these fingers inside of me."

I growled and attacked her mouth, as I slid my hand back to her pussy, sliding her panties to the side and pushing two fingers through her fat lips until they slid inside like she'd asked. I caught her gasp in my mouth and savored her response. Her hips began rising and falling in short waves, and it was all I could do to control my own response against the friction of her rubbing against my cock. *Fuck!* I would not lose control before she did. Adjusting my hand, I rub her clit with my thumb, giving her what she needed. Her legs tightened around my wrist, as she crested toward her release. A loud crash from outside the truck froze us both in place.

"What was that," she said with a whimper, legs instinctively closing, though I was in the way. I looked down at her and could see nervousness overwriting the desire we'd stoked, and I growled in anger. I scanned outside and checked the rearview mirrors as best I could in our position.

"I don't see any..." I trailed off, noticing an almost imperceptible light move behind the tent flaps. "Someone is in the tent." She tried to shift her body to look over her shoulder, and I reluctantly removed my hand. When she sighed, I growled again and kissed her forehead. "We will finish this," I said, helping her move back to the passenger side.

I quietly opened the door and got out of the truck. I walked to the bed and silently grabbed a shovel that was laying back there. I returned to the cab and whispered, "Stay in the truck and call the sheriff."

"Be careful," she whispered back.

Everything after that happened so quickly, I didn't even have time to think. I had barely reached for the tent flap when someone plowed into me, knocking me to the ground. The shovel came out of my hand and landed a few feet from where our bodies lay entangled. I caught my breath and grabbed the attacker's hand before the fist that had been aimed at my face could connect. The guy then tried a headbutt but misjudged our distance in the dark and glided down the side of my face to my shoulder. I took the opportunity to swing my arm up and lock his head in the crook of my neck and shoulder. he thrashed around, trying to get out of the hold. He was taller than me, but he was wiry. I was able to wrap my legs around his legs and tried to use his momentum to flip us both over. I was so focused on trying to get the advantage that I missed his next move, until his elbow connected with my jaw, and I saw stars. My body went slack, and he rolled off me. I could hear his panting in the dwindling awareness.

Get up, Jackson. I heard my own words, though I wasn't sure if I had actually said anything. My head was spinning. I closed my eyes tightly, trying to push away the swirling and its subsequent nausea. *Get up, man.* Where was the guy I was fighting? I could hear his breathing, but whenever I tried to open my eyes, I couldn't see straight, and another wave of nausea would take over. *You gotta get up!* My eyes flew open when the dude straddled my stomach, pinning me to the ground with my arms beneath his knees. Something flickered in the light above the shadow that must have been the man's torso.

"Freddy!"

The guy turned abruptly, and I saw something fly toward his head right before I heard a nasty thud. His weight shifted, and he slipped to the side, leaving only one leg splayed across my waist. Within seconds, Carol's voice broke through the silence and her face came into focus.

"Are you ok? Can you hear me?" She was shaking my shoulders and touching all over my torso.

"Touch lower," I said, though barely a whisper left my lips. I looked into her eyes and smiled.

"You're terrible," she said. "I thought he hurt you. He had a knife."

That got my attention, and I tried to sit up. Dizziness took over, and I flopped flat on my back again. "Shit!"

"Stay there, I hear sirens. We'll get you some help." I did as she said, only because I couldn't do anything else right then. She got up, and I blinked my eyes open to search for her. She was waving at the oncoming emergency vehicles. The guy I'd been fighting was still on the ground near my lower legs. Who in the hell was he, and why had he attacked me? When the sheriff's headlights turned into the parking lot, I got the answer. Freddy's blond hair, coated with red blood, shone in the bright light.

Chapter Nine

CAROL

The next few days passed in a blur of busyness. Though we worked mere yards from each other, I hadn't seen Jackson since he was released from the hospital the day after Freddy's attack. In fact, he didn't come back to work for a full day after his release. Thankfully, the rest of the team had rallied around him and took care of the business side of things, at least that was what Clarissa kept saying. She and Marc had really hit it off, and I smiled thinking of Clarissa settling in with one guy.

The door chime broke me from my thoughts, and Clarissa stormed in.

"Rissa? What's wrong?"

"Men!"

"That's a given, but can you be more specific?"

"Remember how I told you that Marc is shy and quiet, right?" I nodded, waiting for the oncoming tirade. "Well, apparently, those stupid ass man boys over there have started chiding him about spending all his free time with me. I heard those lunkheads mimicking the wedding march when I brought him a coffee after my deliveries."

I couldn't help but chuckle at her indignation. I also knew there would be retribution of some sort and couldn't wait to watch the fireworks. "So how do you plan on getting them back," I asked with a smirk.

"What do you mean?" Clarissa looked genuinely confused by the question. "Get them back?"

"You have never before let a man make you feel uncomfortable without doing something to make him feel even worse. You, my dear, are the queen of holding men accountable."

"When they've done something to me, yes, of course. This isn't about me, though." Her voice cracked, and her breath shuddered. I quickly closed the distance and enveloped her in a hug. I had never seen Clarissa so distraught on someone else's behalf, especially not a man.

"You really like this guy, huh?"

"Yeah, and I hate that others can make him feel uncomfortable about us being together. Do you think he secretly regrets the time we've shared? I don't want him to resent me."

"Whoa, whoa, whoa, missy! I have seen how Marc looks at and looks for you every day. There is not one iota of regret in those looks. He may not like his friends' attention, but he damn sure likes yours. And if he ever opens his mouth to even mimic resentment, I will make him regret it."

"Does he really look for me?"

"All the time. In fact, he was in here earlier asking when you'd be back." Clarissa beamed, and I smiled, instinctively hugging her tighter.

"I want to invite him to Thanksgiving dinner, but you know how my mom is. I don't want him to think I'm embarrassed to have him meet my family, and I don't want him to eat a diner-made turkey dinner in that dusty old hotel room."

"What do you mean? Do they not have plans to go home for the holiday?" Clarissa shook her head. My eyes drifted toward the window to look at the tents. I hadn't even considered that the team would be stuck here, eating takeout in their hotel.

"Jackson didn't tell you?"

I shook my head. "Things have been so busy that I've just gone home and crashed when we've finished up each night. I've hardly seen him, other than occasionally out the window when he's helped customers."

Clarissa pulled away and raised an eyebrow. "The way that man stares in this direction all day, and he hasn't been over here to speak?" I laughed and turned back toward the workroom. "Don't walk away. Seriously, what's the deal between you two?"

"I don't owe you an explanation, Rissa, and I don't know that I have an answer, even if I did. We like each other, I think, but things are complicated, or complications come up. Every time we get a chance to be alone together, something interrupts. It's like the universe is interceding."

"Fuck the universe," she said loudly just as the door chimed. She repeated herself more quietly and went to help the customers who had entered. I watched her for a second, and then gave one last glance outside before getting back to work. At least, I tried to work. I couldn't stop thinking about Clarissa's pained expression. Dammit, that girl could talk me into almost anything without trying.

I walked into the back room and opened the drawer closest to the swinging door. I vaguely remembered dropping Jackson's business card in there when the team first arrived. Hard to believe it had been nearly two weeks. It took forever to find the card in that junk drawer, but I quickly sent off a text before I could change my mind.

> Is it true your team will not be going home for Thanksgiving?

> ...

> Seriously, Jackson. You're planning to eat Thanksgiving dinner alone in your hotel rooms?

> Who is this?

I rolled my eyes, my empathy waning in the midst of his ridiculous question.

> It's Carol. Who else would be asking you about that?

> ...

I seethed when those three dots sat on the screen. He was seriously going to leave me on read with his phone unlocked and not answer. We hadn't spoken in days, days after I had saved his life, and he was just going to ignore me. I had half a mind to walk into the tent, customers be damned, and tell him what I thought about his rudeness. Yes, that was exactly what I'd do. I turned toward the door and walked right into a perfectly formed chest.

I gasped, and he grabbed me before I fell backward. Our eyes locked, and I felt the wind knocked out of me by the intensity of his gaze.

"Dammit, Jackson, stop sneaking in here like a fucking specter!"

"Stop being so oblivious to someone entering your space."

"You take up so much space, I can't be oblivious of your presence." My voice had softened a bit, and I didn't know why. I wanted to still yell at him, maybe bang on his chest, maybe bang out some angry sex on the floor. Reluctantly, I admitted the need for him had not slackened at all.

"Is there a reason why you're provoking me, beautiful."

"Provok... I'm provoking you? You left me on read. I sent you a serious message, and you ignored me."

"I'm standing right here, Carol." He looked down into my eyes and tightened his hold around my waist. "You're still standing in my arms. Does this truly count as ignoring you?"

"Well, no, but..."

He shook his head and leaned down to nuzzle my neck. "No buts when you were the one avoiding me all week."

I tried pulling away from him, but when he took my earlobe between his teeth, my knees went weak, and I dug my fingers into his shoulders. How dare he say something like that and then do this. I tried to think of a way to regain control of the conversation, but my thoughts were pooled between my thighs. Why did we always have to be somewhere public where we'd be interrupted? *No, wait, that's not what I was supposed to be thinking.* I needed to breathe. I needed his mouth. No. *Dammit.*

I managed to blurt, "Are you ever going to answer my question, or are you just going to try and seduce me in my workshop?" He shrugged. The ass actually had the audacity to shrug. "Let go of me, Jackson," I said while pushing into his chest. He smiled and released me.

"No, we do not have any plans for Thursday. No one made plans to go home since that is supposedly the busiest weekend of the season, and we'd have to be back here Friday morning. As for what or where we will eat, I haven't worked that out yet." He spread his arms in a questioning gesture that screamed sarcasm louder than his actual question. "Is my answer to your satisfaction, ma'am?"

"No, sir, it is not. You cannot expect your men to forego a holiday meant for sharing a homemade meal with family and friends because you have failed to plan ahead." He flinched.

Good, I thought. That means he cares. Hopefully, that will make the next part of this conversation go much easier.

"What would you have me do? I don't even know which restaurants, if any, are open. I hardly know anyone here besides my team, you, and Clarissa."

My breath caught, guilt creeping in for trying to gain the upper hand in this manner. I looked down until I could control my breathing again. I would not let him know how contrite I felt at provoking his guilt, at least not aloud, at least not today. I needed him to say yes, and I needed to control my emotions. I would not beg.

"I would have you all over to my house for Thanksgiving dinner. Clarissa has to spend part of the day with her family, but she always feels better when she can escape to my house." I reached out and grabbed his shoulder. "Please don't say anything." His mouth was slightly ajar, not with surprise or sarcasm but rather incredulity. "Don't look at me like that. Clarissa was nearly in tears as she was telling me about you all potentially having to eat in the hotel. Why didn't you say something?"

Chapter Ten

JACKSON

I hadn't known what to say when Carol asked me to bring the men to dinner at her house. What was I supposed to say to her accusation that I hadn't planned ahead? I hadn't had a chance to plan for anything in this gods-forsaken situation. My grandfather certainly hadn't given me a head's up about anything, so I was flying this skeleton of a plane. Not only had one of my men tried to rape a woman in town, he'd damn near killed me while Carol watched. The only thing I felt secure about was the all-encompassing desire for this woman who went from scorching hot to frigid in minutes, leaving me blistered. All I could manage was a convoluted apology when she'd asked why I hadn't said anything.

"When you avoided me since I was discharged from the hospital, I figured you didn't want anything more to do with me. Then you text..."

It felt ridiculous. I wanted her to see me at my best, and I hadn't shown much more than the worst. Yet, she still invited us to her house. I didn't understand her, but that didn't stop me from the pull I felt toward her. Even as I was counting out the till and preparing to close down the shop, I had the urge to walk back through her door and pull her back into my arms. I wanted a second chance at our bar date. I wanted her back on my lap and to forget any of these responsibilities and insecurities. Why couldn't life just be simple?

"Hey boss." Marc was standing less than 5 feet away.

When had he come back inside the tent? They had been locking everything down outside.

"What's up?" I closed the cash box and zipped the deposit bag. I'd drop that off on the way to the hotel tonight. We'd made far more this week than any of us could've imagined.

"We're almost out of Frasier. Do you think the old man will send us another shipment before Thursday?"

"I'll call him tomorrow and let him know." I hated the idea of calling Nick. I still wasn't over the abrupt way he'd exiled me down the mountain away from the family and left to drown with an unpracticed team. I might never forgive the old man.

"Ok then. We're all locked up. The guys want to run out to the pub before heading to the hotel. You good with Travis driving the truck?"

"You're not going with them?" I could guess the answer, but still, I felt responsible for these guys and wanted to know their plans.

"Nah. Clarissa and I are going to watch a movie. I don't even know what's playing, but we got plans."

My brows just about lifted off my head. I could only imagine what those two had planned for a near-empty dark theater on a random Monday night.

"Don't get arrested," I said, and Marc's smile spread across his face. "Tell the other guys it's fine, but they better not get arrested either."

"I'm on it, boss." Marc turned to leave, but I called him back.

"Oh yeah, Carol has invited us all to her house for Thanksgiving dinner with her and Clarissa. It appears our florist friends didn't like the idea of our team getting takeout turkey."

Marc beamed, and I waved him away. They all deserved some fun. It had been a crazy busy week, and it didn't seem to be slowing. In the city, I didn't know anyone who put their Christmas tree up before Thanksgiving. Apparently, there's some kind of tradition here in the sticks. That thought reminded me of the pending call up the mountain for more trees. My mood, buoyed by Marc's joy, immediately sobered.

I exited the tent and looked across the lot to the floral shop. It was already dark, and both women's cars were gone. *Damn.*

Chapter Eleven

JACKSON

Whence I got back to the hotel, my mind would not let me sleep. I was torn about my feelings for Carol and the discomfort of tomorrow's phone call. I didn't know whether my grandfather had heard everything that had happened at Ardor Point over the past week or not. After tossing and turning for an hour, I picked up my phone thinking to scroll through social media, something to pass the time and possibly lull me to sleep. But when I put the screen in front of my face, the first thing that showed up was Carol's text.

I hadn't closed out of it before deciding to barge into her workshop. I wished I could read her roller-coaster emotions better. Unlike with my Diane, I had no doubt that Carol's emotions were genuine, but it didn't help me know where I stood with her. I also didn't understand why this attraction was so strong. We hardly knew each other. Yet, there I lay, phone in hand, looking at her display of anger, wishing I could touch her.

"She's probably asleep," I said to the empty room. "Which is where I should be," I said aloud to myself. I sighed and laid the phone on my chest, closing my eyes and hoping sleep would find me. A moment later, my phone vibrated, making me jump. Heart racing, I went to unlock the screen. Then anxiety filled my chest. It was late. What if something was wrong? No one would contact me this late unless something was wrong. It wasn't until the phone vibrated a second time that I worked up the nerve to unlock it.

> Are you up?

My heart leapt. I looked around the room. Was I asleep and had conjured her in my dreams? I looked at the phone again and there were those three dots saying another message was coming.

> ...

The wait, though only a few seconds, was excruciating. Would she leave me waiting like I'd left her?

Yes, I'm up.

Still those three dots teased me. What was she doing? Did she send a message and then fall asleep? I closed my eyes again, trying to calm my mind when the phone buzzed. I took a deep breath and lifted it. There on the screen was an entire wall of text, and my chest tightened.

I knew what a wall of text from a woman meant. It meant they were tired of my shit. It meant they were done with me. It meant I'd never get a chance to correct whatever it was that I had done wrong. I learned that lesson from my mother, and it was thoroughly reviewed by my ex, and a few others before her. Tension built in my neck, and I knew a headache wasn't far behind. I punched in the words 'I'm sorry' with my thumb and put the phone on the bedside table.

It was fun while it lasted, I thought. As if this whole trip out here couldn't get any worse. The phone immediately started buzzing. Not the single buzz of a text message but the repeated droning of a phone call. I ignored it at first and when it stopped ringing, I sighed, but it started again. I grabbed the phone and, without even looking, connected. "What," I barked at whoever was on the other end.

"Jackson? Are you ok?"

That voice. That was the voice that had slipped into my dreams for the past two weeks. She had just sent me an angry text. Why did she sound worried?

"Are you still there?" I stared at the ceiling, unable to find my words. "Hey, you're making me worried. Not to sound like the hulk or anything, but you won't like me when I'm worried."

I couldn't suppress a laugh. It bubbled up from inside of me. She was worried about me, not angry. "I thought you were mad at me," I said quietly.

"Why should I be mad at you? Have you done something since your stealthy entrance into my workshop?"

I laughed again. The ice that had started to form in my chest began melting. "I don't think so," I said. "You just sent me a whole wall of text at damn near midnight."

"Did you even read it before you apologized, Jackson?" There was something in her voice that made me sit up like I had missed something important. "Jackson?"

"Give me a second." I went through the motions of opening the text app.

> Look, I haven't talked about myself or my past before I came here with anyone beside my best friend, but I think you deserve some kind of explanation for my behavior. I realize I have been a bit inconsistent in my response to you. No one deserves that, and you haven't done anything to warrant it, other than being new, extremely sexy, and quite frustrating, honestly. But you are not the reason I keep freezing up.

I sat there. I knew I needed to say something because she was waiting for me to come back on the phone, but there was a knot in my throat. She had been apologizing to me, trying to explain herself, and I was...

"I'm an absolute idiot," I said into the phone after I was able to clear my throat.

"Why did you apologize, Jackson?" Her voice was barely a whisper. Its softness clung to me.

"Promise you won't laugh," I asked. I didn't know if I could handle her laughter.

'Tell me' were her only words.

"In my experience, the only time a woman sends a wall of text that begins with the word 'look' in the middle of the night is because it's a Dear John letter. It's because I've fucked up majorly somehow." I sat in silence waiting. The seconds ticking painfully.

"Look, Jackson." She giggled. "See, I start lots of phrases with look. Seriously, though, I don't talk a lot, at least not about myself. Sometimes I find it easier to write out my thoughts and feelings. And sometimes, I have to send them all at once or I will change my mind and delete the whole thing."

I pushed the air I was holding out of my nose, and it came out as a snort because I was trying to hold in a laugh. "I wish I would've known that ten minutes ago."

"Yeah, well, I wish that we had met maybe ten years ago.

But who knows, we might not have liked each other much then."

"So, where do we go from here," I asked. I'd have said just about anything to keep her talking. Her voice was a balm on my heart and lit a fire in my soul.

"Where would you like this to go, Jackson? You're here for a season."

She was right. My time in Ardor Point was temporary. I hadn't thought about relocating any time soon. In fact, I hadn't thought beyond needing to get out of California and away from the drama haunting my life. I didn't know what I wanted beyond the moment, so I told her the truth. She didn't hang up on me. Instead, she shared more about herself.

She had been an adventurous woman at one time. Relationships were consensual and mutually advantageous, or they ended. We each shared our thoughts on lots of things, including relationships and sex. I damn near choked on my own spit when she said she'd been celibate for ten years, especially after she told me she'd been open to different kinks and had loved being spanked. I found myself rubbing my cock through my boxers while she told her story. What I wouldn't give to see her bare ass turned pink by my hand. I asked if she'd ever been tied up, and she admitted to delving into bondage, on the giving and receiving ends.

All of that ended with David. He had come in and swept her off her feet and then ruined her. She didn't give many details, but I sobered by the serious turn of the conversation, imagining something terrible had happened. It was enough to not only bring the cosmopolitan city girl to the country but to also leave her voluntarily celibate rather than have someone else touch her.

"Thank you for sharing more of yourself with me. You didn't have to do that. Are you willing to tell me what your hard limits are should we ever get to that point?"

"No choking is the big one. Otherwise, if you listen in the moment, I will tell you when something is too much."

I willingly agreed before we got off the phone, grateful that she still considered the possibility of me getting her alone. I'd honestly have agreed to anything for the chance. I wanted to have her purring in my arms again, giving her pleasure in the way she liked. Her revelations weren't as surprising as they might have been had I not witnessed her tasting her own juices from my fingers. The memory of her telling me to finger her had me rock hard. I reached for my cock, replaying the moments she'd melted into my arms and the taste of her mouth. I wanted to taste all of her.

My strokes increased in speed as I thought about having her over my lap again, this time face down. *She liked to be spanked, huh?* Though she kept her ass covered in those billowy skirts of hers, I'd watched her enough to know it would jiggle beautifully when my hand connected to it. My hand took on a mind of its own as my thoughts wandered to a plan for Thanksgiving night. I'd get Clarissa to help me empty the house. Then I'd get a tour of it and every inch of Carol. No sooner had I imagined having her in the shower, soap lather running down our bodies, I groaned in release. Sleep came immediately after.

I woke with a smile on my face, still happy from last night's conversation with Carol. I showered and was dressing when dread broke through the bliss. I picked up the phone and dialed Nick's number. I knew the old man would be awake already. Sleeping in was a sin. So was punishing a child for the sins of his parents, but that wasn't an argument I would win.

"You ready to tell me what the hell is going on down there, boy?" I took a deep breath and schooled my emotions. Though the old man couldn't see me, I did not want to show anything besides confidence through my voice.

"We had a great week of sales this week, and we need more

Fraziers. We could probably use a few extra dozen Douglases as well."

"You know that's not what I meant." His voice was ice. It still startled me how differently my grandfather addressed me now from the warmth he'd exuded 30 years ago. "Why were the cops on my lot...twice?"

My anger flashed hot at that accusation. If anyone was at fault for the events from last week, it was the old man. "One of the men you hired attacked a server at the diner. He then tried to rob us before trying to kill me."

"Don't blame that on me, boy. I left you in charge of the team."

"You left me to fail with this misfit team. What happened to the regular seasonal workers? What happened to setting your crew up for success. You abandoned us down here. I hadn't been to Ardor Point since I was a kid."

The old man's breathing was haggard. I could hear his anger mounting, but I was ready for it. I wanted to know what grudge I was being punished for.

"You chose not to come back! You abandoned us," Nick spat out, his voice low with venom.

"I came here now and look at how you're treating me. I don't know what the hell I did wrong, but look at how you're treating your team, your business, to somehow try and punish me." My breath was heavy with emotion, anger returning in a tsunami. "You know what, try your best, old man! Send the damn trees or don't, we will clear this lot, and then you can answer for why we ran out." I pressed the end call button and threw the phone onto the chair across the room.

I sat there with my head in my hands for what felt like an hour until someone knocked on the door. I looked up but didn't move. My breathing had calmed, and the anger had dissipated, but I was left hollow.

"Boss, you ok in there?" Marc's voice came through the door. "I already took everyone to the lot, and when you didn't show up, I called. You didn't answer, so I came back. You good, man?"

I liked Marc. The kid was good with numbers, worked hard to keep everyone straight, and genuinely cared about the team. I just wasn't in the mood to see anyone yet. "I'm good. I'll be there in a bit. Had to call about the trees."

"Ok, cool. See you there."

Chapter Twelve

CAROL

I woke up early. Normally, I'd sleep in a bit on Thanksgiving, as it would be my last day off until Christmas Day, but I was having company. *I was having company.* I had to keep reminding myself. I needed time to get the food done and clean. I couldn't depend on Clarissa's help until early afternoon. The poor girl was stuck pretending their family was a happy, healthy unit until the meal was served. Then she usually showed up here to decompress. Miel meowed from the other side of the bedroom door, and I groaned. No matter the desire to stay in bed, it was definitely time to get up.

I prepped the turkey and set to cleaning. I wanted everything to be perfect. This was the first time I'd have anyone beside Clarissa in my house in years. The hostess training kicked back in immediately. Work top to bottom, one room at a time, and do the bathroom last after showers were done. I'd take care of that this afternoon after I had help to finish up the final items.

By the time Clarissa arrived, I had already set up the dining area, taken out the turkey, set up the dessert bar, and prepped the deviled eggs. "You're on mashed potato duty," I said and headed toward the bathroom.

"Hello to you too," Clarissa yelled at my back. I could hear the smile in her voice and appreciated her understanding. As I undressed, Jackson sent a text asking if they needed to bring anything. I smiled at the phone and almost left it unanswered.

BYOB

Gotcha! See you soon!

Classical music penetrated the house as Clarissa made herself at home in the kitchen. I dressed quickly in a tight orange dress that complimented my shape and my hair. I was showing off a little, but I didn't really feel the hostess part in my normal everyday attire. When I walked into the kitchen scrunching waves into my short, wet hair, Clarissa whistled.

"Damn, Carol, I didn't think you had it in you to wear something that actually fit in front of the guys." She elongated the last word, emphasizing the z sound at the end. I shook my head and laughed.

"I haven't hosted a dinner party in years. We'll see if I remember what in the hell I'm doing."

"Well, you sure look the part, and the house looks great!"

I began pulling all the cold items out of the fridge and taking them to the table. There weren't any servants, so we would do this family style with everything on the table to be passed around. The dining room wasn't big enough to set out a buffet. The table with its necessary extra leaves took up too much space.

"Holy shit, C. Have you ever opened this table up all the way before?"

I gave her a look of 'what do you think?'. We finished putting out all the food, Clarissa moved the music from her phone to the TV surround sound, so it could give ambience, and we awaited our guests. When the guys arrived, I had a moment where I wanted to run and hide in the bedroom. A flash of memory of five men walking into the house with just me and another woman hit me, and I had to quickly push it away. Jackson's smile helped.

"It smells wonderful in here." He hugged me, and before I could pull away, he whispered, "you look wonderful." I blushed and greeted everyone else.

The six of us sat around the large dining room table in relative silence at the start of the meal. Travis asked to say Grace, and I used the opportunity to look at Jackson through my lowered lashes. He was looking back at me, and a streak of heat ran down my stomach and into my lap. He smirked at my blush, and I kicked him under the table. He silently mouthed a promise for retribution, and my brows rose in challenge. Marc interrupted our moment by breaking the silence as everyone dug into the platters of food.

"Thank you for inviting us over, Carol. This is far nicer than the hotel lobby." The other men nodded in agreement.

"Yes, thank you for opening your home," Jackson said, his eyes boring into mine. My breath caught at the heat in his stare.

"I only wish I'd have known sooner and could have prepared something more. You all have been wonderful to have around this year," I said, looking around the table, trying to keep myself from staring at Jackson. I would not be a very good hostess if all my attention was on one person.

"Something more?" Peter asked, his gaze lingering on the dessert table off to the side. "I don't know how you did all this and kept the flower shop open all day every day."

"She has help," Marc said with a hint of impatience.

Peter is usually the quiet one, so I wondered at Marc's

response. Then, I watched him take Clarissa's hand under the table and smile. I made a mental note to ask Clarissa about that expression of jealousy. A little possessiveness is nice, but it can quickly escalate to something dark. Not that I worry about Clarissa seeing through any ulterior motives. She's been living with those types of behaviors her whole life.

"I, honestly, could not make it through the holidays without Clarissa," I say to clear the tension. "It also helped to have all of you on the lot because I felt comfortable leaving her alone for longer than I would normally."

"Glad to help," Jackson chimed in before shoveling in a mouthful of food. He had looked like he wanted to say something more and then realized we weren't alone.

The rest of dinner passed by in a contented blur. The young guys bantered back and forth. Clarissa grabbed Marc's hand a couple times when things got too personal, and she even elbowed travis in the side once for an inappropriate comment. I didn't track all of the words exchanged because I was too engrossed in Jackson's heated gaze. What started off as the occasional glance, soon turned panty-drenching stares. I was so focused on my thoughts of Jackson's mouth that I nearly choked when Peter and Travis asked about trying my cookies.

When the meal ended, I sent them to the living room to watch the game. Marc and Jackson offered to help clean up, but I shooed them away. I even sent Clarissa out of the kitchen to spend time with her man. I needed a few minutes alone to breathe and take it all in. I'd survived my first dinner party with only a moment of genuine anxiety. My therapist bestie would be proud of me. I'd have to call her this weekend and give her all the details.

I was moving dishes from the sink into the dishwasher when strong hands grabbed my hips and pulled me against him. I held in a gasp, as my mind reeled and threatened to bring forth a slew of terrible images. Then I heard his voice and relaxed.

"Need some help?"

I stood up straight and leaned back into Jackson. He wrapped his arms around me and held me close. He pressed his face into my hair, and then kissed my head softly. I slid my hand up and cupped around the back of his head, leaning my head to the side, giving him access to my neck. He took the hint and kissed me behind the earlobe and then again lower into the crease where my neck and shoulder meet. I sighed and turned to face him. His brown eyes bore into mine, and I took a deep breath. He took advantage of my open mouth and ravaged it with his own. Our tongues touched, and my panties were a goner. Kissing him was enough to set tremors off between my thighs. He released my mouth and returned to my neck.

"Jackson." It wasn't a statement or a question. It was an invitation. I wanted everything he had to give.

"Hmmm." He lifted his head and smiled. "I'd wanted to do that since I stepped foot in the house and saw you. That dress is killer." He grabbed my hand, lifted it, and twirled me around in front of him. "Then I came in here, and you were bent over." He shook his head and whistled softly.

I blushed. "Hush, or they'll hear you out there."

"Who?" My eyes widened. He smirked. "There's nobody here but us."

"Jackson? I didn't even come out to say goodbye. That's terrible."

"Nobody thinks it's terrible. In fact, they wished me well on their way out the door."

I slapped his chest playfully. "You're terrible."

"And you're delicious. I plan to taste every inch of you tonight, so finish those dishes." He turned me around and gave my ass a swat. I jumped and felt my knees get weak. The dishwasher had never been filled that quickly before.

"Good, now take off that dress."

I looked at Jackson over my shoulder. Something about his command sent tingles down my spine, and they weren't from fear. His eyes were on my ass. I reached behind my back and grabbed the zipper of my dress. I slowly pulled it down, exposing my back inch by inch. I lifted my right heel and started to take off my shoe.

"No, leave those on."

His voice was a hoarse whisper that sent tendrils of heat down my stomach. I looked back at him again, and his eyes caught mine. He was leaning against the island with his legs crossed at the ankles. His arousal was evident through his slacks. I bit my lower lip. He looked down at the dress and then back into my eyes, a warning that only added to my arousal. His silent appraisal was turning me on even more than his words. I dropped the dress from my shoulders and let it fall to the floor. I heard his breath catch and smiled.

I stepped out of the dress and slowly bent to pick it up. A growl left his throat, and he was pulling me back into him before I could even stand up. I made to turn around and face him, but he held me still. His hand reached down to palm my already juicy lips.

"Already wet for me, Carol?" His breath was warm against my ear, and I shivered with desire. He found my clit through my panties and began making circles with his finger. A moan escaped my throat. I reached up and grabbed around his neck again, this time more to hold myself upright than anything seductive. He breathed my name out onto my neck. My whole body lit on fire, and I moaned in delight at the sensations he was creating.

"I want to try something," he said quietly.

'Hmm' was all I could manage in reply.

"There are so many things I want to do to you, but first, I want to blindfold you."

I froze. Why would he want me blindfolded? He told me no one else was here. Was that a ploy?

"Carol?" He pulled his hand off of me and turned me to face him. "Hey, what's the matter?"

I couldn't bring myself to look at his face. I was afraid of what I might see. "Why do I need to be blindfolded?"

He lifted my chin with his finger and stared straight into my eyes. "I will not hurt you."

"Why did everyone leave without saying goodbye?"

Confusion clouded his eyes, before his gaze softened. He grabbed my hand and led me around the island toward the kitchen door. He gestured for me to open it. My heart rate rose, and my breath quickened. I reached a trembling hand toward the swinging door and pushed it outward. No noises came from the room. I didn't even hear Miel purring for attention. I took a step into the doorway and peaked my head out around it. No one was there. I walked across the room and looked through the window on the front door. Clarissa's car and the other truck were gone. I let out a steadying breath before turning to look back at Jackson.

His head tilted to the side, but he didn't say anything. I gave him a sheepish smile and felt my cheeks get hot. I hated that I had to question everything. It was so unfair to him. Yet, there he stood looking at me with compassion and understanding. He had somehow understood the reason for my apprehension, and I was grateful. I closed the distance between us and quickly pulled down his head for a kiss. When we pulled apart, his eyes were again dark with desire, but there was a knowing smile on his face.

Jackson reached into his pocket and pulled out a long piece of cloth. He let it dangle from his fingers in front of me. I looked at him for a long moment before nodding and putting my back to him, so he could tie the cloth in place. Once I assured him that I could not see anything, he whispered in my ear. "This is all for you." I smiled at the resurgence of heat that came from his breath on my skin.

He trailed his hands down the sides of my neck and the length of my cleavage before cupping my breasts. I rested my head on his shoulder. "Do you know what I have been thinking about repeatedly since our conversation the other night?" I had no idea what he was talking about. I could barely think with him touching me. He slowly walked me over toward the couch.

"What," I asked when I felt him sit down.

He leaned forward and kissed my abdomen right above my panty line. I had expected to be more self-conscious about him seeing me naked for the first time. I'd always been a thick girl, and never had any hang-ups about my weight, but I'd gained some pounds since the last time I'd been naked in front of a man. Jackson did not seem to mind as he explored my midsection. I began to mind when heat pooled in the area below where he was kissing.

"I've imagined you over my lap, and your beautiful ass turning pink beneath my hand."

I barely had time to bite my lip before he pulled me down across his legs. He grabbed my knees that were dangling off the couch, and pulled them up onto the cushions, so my ass was angled up. He rubbed my ass softly and brought his hand down in a light smack. He was teasing me, and I knew it. I waited for the sting I knew would soon come. He did not make me wait long. I moaned in pleasure the first time he pulled my panties out of the way, and his hand connected with my bare ass. His dick twitched under my stomach, and I smiled in anticipation of all that was to come. When he started listing the reasons I deserved the spanking, my pussy pulsed with each stinging slap.

"You've been naughty today." He lowered my panties completely, bringing them down to the middle of my thighs. "You wore that dress, just to make my dick hard." *thwack*

"Rather than just following directions in the kitchen, you decided to tease me with the sexy slow reveal." *thwack* "You didn't trust me when I said we were alone." *thwack* "You've made me wait this long to get you naked." *thwack* My breathing was ragged, and my legs were shaking by the time he was done.

He rolled me over on his lap and placed one of the decorative pillows under my head. Then he slipped the blindfold off. I looked at him wide-eyed, but he said nothing. He slid a hand between my legs and plunged two fingers into my slit. My body offered no resistance, and I moaned his name.

"Come for me," he said, watching my face.

I exploded in ecstasy, but he gave no reprieve. My body was tingling from head to toe, as my walls pulsed with pleasure. Still, he kept moving his fingers in and out of me until I screamed, my body shuddering.

"Good girl."

When my breathing finally stabilized, and I could feel my legs again, I reached for his shoulder and tried to sit up. His cock had been pressing into me, teasing me with its hardness, and I wanted to get my hands on it. The intensity of Jackson's gaze stopped me, and he shook his head. "I'm not done with you yet."

Chapter Thirteen

JACKSON

I was in awe of her. The softness of her skin, the heat of her inner walls, the sounds of her pleasure. I couldn't get enough. Her pulsing in my hand, squeezing my fingers as they plundered for her treasure almost did me in, but I managed to control my body's desire for release. I wanted her pleasure more than I wanted my own. I wanted to erase those terrible memories from her mind and replace them with ecstasy. When she tried to sit up, I was afraid to let her go, afraid she'd pull away from me again.

I stared into her beautiful hazel eyes, hoping she could read my feelings without me having to say a word. I needed to taste her. Without breaking eye contact, I pulled out my fingers and brought them to my lips. I watched her pupils dilate and felt myself twitch with desire. Fuck, she was sexy as hell. I ran my tongue between my fingers, watching her watching me enjoy every drop of her release. I put the fingers in my mouth and sucked off her juices. A deep groan started low in my chest as the desire to devour her took over.

"I need to taste you. I want you screaming my name as I drink up every delicious drop."

I readjusted myself on the couch, lifting the leg closest to my chest until I could settle myself between her legs. With one knee on the floor and other on the couch, I savored the image of her open to me, ready for me to slide inside her. I caressed her breasts with my hands, running my calloused palms over her nipples until they were taut. I then replaced one of my hands with my mouth, and she sighed. I quickly switched between the two mounds, giving equal attention to both. When I ran my teeth over the tight nubs, she hissed with plea-sure, grabbed my hair and held me close. I teased her with my tongue and teeth.

She watched as I made my way down her abdomen, licking and kissing each inch. Her breath was quickening again, and I reveled in her response to my touch. I stopped my descent right below her belly button, and she bit her lower lip. I stayed there waiting for her. "Tell me what you want, Carol." I remembered how seductively she'd answered that question in my truck the last time I'd gotten to touch her, and I wanted her answer now. She locked eyes with me but said nothing. I kissed her lower abdomen, and she shuddered. Still, I didn't move further. When she remained silent, holding my gaze, I dipped my head, and ran my tongue around her belly button. She squirmed beneath me, and I grabbed her hips. "Tell me," I said, my voice hoarse with the restraint I was struggling to maintain.

"Jackson." Her voice was breathy. I knew it was a plea, but I wanted her words.

"Tell me." I slid my hands from her hips, down around her ass, grabbing tightly.

"Fuck," she said with a groan. "Taste me, Jackson."

I used the grasp I already had on her ass and lifted her to

my mouth. My tongue quickly slipped between her lips and found her swollen clit. She tasted like heaven. I swirled my tongue around, and she writhed beneath me. My hands held her steady as I assaulted her most sensitive spot. I licked and sucked until she dug her fingers into my hair and pulled me in closer. Surrounded by the taste and smell of her, I growled. My desire to break her control was primal. I lifted her hips higher until I could slide my tongue inside her. At the sound of her gasp, I fucked her with my mouth. I looked up to see her squeezing her nipples, and I growled again, licking my way back up to her clit.

"Oh my god, Jackson, please!"

I shifted slightly and slid two fingers back inside her as I continued my pressured assault on her clit. I felt her slick walls tightening around my fingers, and her clit stiffened.

"Yes, yes, yes," she repeated multiple times until she fell silent. I smiled and leaned my head against her thigh. I kissed her lips and tenderly licked down her slit, pulling out my fingers, so I could drink her nectar.

"Mmmmm." I reached down to pull out my throbbing cock when someone pounded on the door.

Carol rolled off the couch to the floor. I grabbed her shoulder before she could run off and put my finger to my lips. We would just ignore the knock.

"Boss! Carol! Jackson, answer the door."

I scowled. What the fuck was Marc doing back here? He should be busy with Clarissa. I had told Marc I'd get a ride back to the hotel with Carol in the morning, but he'd decided to leave the other truck anyway. There was no need for him to be here.

"Carol?" That was Clarissa's voice. Carol looked up at me, and I handed her one of the throws she kept on the back of the couch.

"Let me see what's going on." I stood and adjusted my balls. Though the interruption had softened my erection some, things were still uncomfortably out of place. I opened the door a crack and growled at our two assistants. "The damn shops better be on fire!" Carol giggled behind me, and I scowled at them even more deeply. Their interruption was unwanted and untimely.

"Sorry to interrupt, boss, but you need to come to the hotel now."

"Yeah, you're going to want to leave," Clarissa said in an ominous tone as she pushed past me and entered the house.

"What is going on," Carol called to me after Clarissa had passed the threshold. I wondered the same thing.

Marc leaned in and whispered, "A woman named Diane is there claiming to be your fiancé."

I closed my eyes and took a deep breath. *Shit.* What was she doing here? How'd she even know where to find me? I leaned back around the door and looked at Carol. Clarissa was sitting on the couch next to her with a hand on Carol's shoulder. Clarissa stared daggers at me.

"Is it true, boss? Are you engaged?"

I didn't say a word, just exited the house and climbed in the passenger side of the truck. I should've known better. Every time my life seemed to take a turn for the better, something, or someone, came along and fucked it up even worse.

"Fuck," I yelled and pounded my fist on the dash. I probably would have kept yelling, but I saw Marc flinch. I put my head in my hands and fell silent again.

Chapter Fourteen

JACKSON

I entered the hotel lobby like a man on a mission. How dare that bitch show up here? I looked around and my eye caught the flash of a platinum ponytail surrounded by my team. I would not let her get her claws into any of them. They all deserved better than her. I walked up behind Travis, but my eyes never left Diane. She was laughing at something, and my stomach recoiled at the sound. I used to love her laugh. It was full and bright. Watching her now, I realized that laugh never reached her eyes. They were as dull and devoid of emotion as they had been the day before I left town. The only time she ever showed true emotion was in the throes of passion.

"What are you doing here," I asked through gritted teeth.

"Jackson, darling. I'm so glad you're here!" She stood, and the men slid their chairs back to let her through. Her smile grew wider as she approached me, and my anger grew deeper with each of her steps. "I've missed you," she said, putting her hands up, as if to put them around my neck.

I took a step back and grabbed her hands, pushing them back down to her sides. "Answer my question, Diane. What are you doing here? How did you know where to find me?" I kept my voice low. Everyone in this small town didn't need to know my business, and I didn't want my men looking at me any more differently than they likely were since her arrival.

"Your grandfather is just like Santa Claus, and he gifted me the information. It wasn't hard to find your family name in this area, though I'll admit driving up the mountain was, um, interesting." I saw her smile fade and knew she was repulsed by the lack of what she would consider civilization up there on the mountain. She probably didn't think much more highly of Ardor Point in the short time she'd been here.

"Go home, Diane."

"Oh, come now, Jackson. It's Thanksgiving. I wanted to spend the holiday with you." Her voice raised, so that everyone around could hear her words. Of course, she'd want a spectacle.

My eyebrows shot up, but I moved in closer to her. "What game are you playing?"

She put her lips to my ear, "Why don't we go somewhere private, and I'll let you play too."

I gritted my teeth to the point my gums ached, but then I stepped away from her and smiled at my crew. "Thank you all for entertaining Diane until I could get here. Obviously, I didn't know she was going to fly all the way out here from California." I looked each of them in the eye, hoping they could read how uncomfortable I was with this whole situation. I couldn't read most of their faces. Only Marc looked at me with sympathy. At least, one of them knew I wasn't a total asshole.

"This way," I said and held out my arm for Diane to take. As soon as we were in the elevator, I moved as far away from her as possible. She turned toward me and smiled like the predator she was. As we began moving upward, she stalked toward me, unbuttoning her silk blouse, so I could see her cleavage. It was amply displayed in her customary pushup bra. I was disgusted with myself for ever having imagined anything genuine about her. She was plastic through and through.

"You know you've missed me, Jackson," she purred as she got close enough to run her hand up my chest." Before I could respond, verbally or physically, she reached up and gripped my hair, pulling my lips down to hers. She pulled away, eyes large and bright, and then her lip curled into a sneer. "Who is she?"

I was so surprised by the whole thing that I barely schooled my expression at her question. My mind reeled. *Fuck!* She'd really be on the prowl now, and I wouldn't be the only one left scarred. "None of your business," I managed to say with a snarl. She smiled and turned back toward the elevator door as it opened. I did not want to be alone with this woman, but I had no choice for the moment, so I led the way to my room.

"You've been a naughty boy, Jackson," she said with a lecherous grin. "You should have brought her back here with you. We could have had some fun."

"You know damn well that is not my idea of fun."

"Yes, I remember how selfish you are. Your mother warned me about that side of you, but I thought she was wrong. I thought you'd do anything for me. Isn't that what people are supposed to do for those they love."

I could feel my anger rise. My mother was a fine one to call someone else selfish. She'd taken me away from everyone who'd actually loved me, or at least shown me love. She'd kept me from coming back to my grandparents and then isolated me from my father. She'd used me as a pawn. Diane wanted to do the same thing. Unfortunately, it had taken me too long to see it. "My mother is the wrong one to get advice from, but you two are like peas in a pod."

She laughed. "What a quaint saying. You are obviously in your element here in this sleepy town at the base of that mountain wilderness your grandfather calls a home."

"You're such a snob."

"And a bitch according to our last conversation. But you know my favorite position has always been doggy. Come on, Jackson, let's not fight." She backed me into the wall. She'd always been the dominant one in our relationship, especially sexually. Something about her aggressive desire always turned me on, and I could feel my wayward dick tightening, the traitorous bastard.

She turned around and rubbed her ass on my groin, and my breath hitched. She grabbed my hands and pulled them up to cup her breast. A groaned slipped from my throat. *Dammit!* My body was not listening to my brain. When she stuck my fingers in her mouth and sucked, my dick jumped.

"Mmmmmm." She let my hand drop back down to her waist, and she turned around to face me. I stiffened under her discerning gaze. "Tell me something, Jackson." She nuzzled my neck beneath my chin. I said nothing. I knew there would eventually be a question, and it wouldn't be a good one. Still, the feel of her tongue tracing up my neck, over my chin, and around my lips made me close my eyes as a wave of desire crashed into me. I grabbed her hips and pulled her against my hard shaft. It was aching to be set free. I'd gone too long and been too close too many times today. She sucked on each of my lips separately, and then her tongue darted into my mouth to dance with mine. I moaned again.

She stopped and looked up at me. The light shining in her eye was unnerving and I let her go. She looked down my body. "I just want to know," she said, as she reached down and cupped me through my slacks. She unbuttoned the pants and slipped her hand inside. "Did she taste as good when your face was between her legs, as she still does now on your lips and fingers?" I tried to push her away, but she grabbed tighter onto my cock, her nails grazing the shaft.

I hissed. "What the fuck is wrong with you?" She had absolutely no boundaries. There was no length she would not go to get what she wanted.

"What's wrong with me is that you are not fucking me."

I scowled, pulled her hand from my pants and went to sit on the couch. "You did not come all this way, drive up and back down a mountain in a rental, and entertain my blue-collar crew because you weren't getting fucked."

"That's not the point. I want you too." She got on her knees in front of me and grabbed my hands. "Jackson, we worked well together. We looked good together. Our engagement was a buzz. I want that energy back." If I didn't know how good of an actress she was, I'd have believed her pleas, though ridiculous and selfish, were genuine. I had no doubt she wanted the spotlight, but she didn't want me.

"Find someone else. Hell, find ten someones. I'm not interested in the spotlight or you." I pulled my hands out of hers before getting up and walking over to the hotel phone.

"What are you doing?"

"Hello...Yes...Are there any rooms available for tonight?... Great!...Please just charge that room's rate to my account...I'll be sending someone down to get the key...Her name is Diane." I looked at her from the corner of my eye, and I could feel the anger emanating off her.

"You're going to regret this, Jackson. I'll make sure you're never welcomed back into our circle again."

"Do you have a return ticket home for tomorrow? If not, I suggest you go ahead and call to change your return flight."

She was seething now. I could see it so clearly. How I'd ever missed this side of her before, I didn't know. Her fists were clenched, and her eyes shot daggers at me. "Go get your room, Diane, and have a safe trip home."

She screeched, and I prepared myself for her attack, but then she smiled and stormed out the door. I shuddered.

I walked in the bathroom and turned on the shower. I needed to wash her presence away and clear my head. As soon as the water hit my skin, my thoughts turned to Carol. *Dammit!* How was I going to fix things?

Chapter Fifteen
CAROL

I sat on the floor in front of the couch wrapped in my throw. Clarissa went into the kitchen to make us each a cup of tea. I heard her complain about the lack of coffee. If I hadn't been so miserable, I would have laughed. I couldn't believe Jackson had hidden the fact he had a girlfriend. No, not just a girlfriend, a fiancé. Guilt washed over me. I never wanted to be the other woman or a home wrecker. I had half a mind to call him and tell him what I thought of him and his omissions, but that would only make me feel worse with the fiancé there. I could run him over the coals tomorrow.

Clarissa handed me the steaming cup and sat on the couch.

"Don't give me that look, Rissa. I don't need your sympathy. I'm a grown woman."

"Grown or not, you're still hurt. I see it in your eyes." Clarissa put her hand on my shoulder.

I snorted. "I don't want to talk about it."

"Carol, you listen to me all the time. You need to talk to someone. It is not good to keep all this shit boxed up in your head. Talk to me. I'm here for you. I stayed because I knew as soon as I saw the snooty bitch..." I shot her a scathing look. "Well, she was. Anyway, I knew as soon as she introduced herself and asked for him that you would be the one left hurt in this situation."

"I feel guilty for pursuing a taken man, Riss." I looked up at her with tears. "It had been such a long time since I'd even felt the slightest attraction for a man, I didn't even bother to ask if he had anyone at home."

"Don't take on that guilt. You are not a mind reader. That was for him to tell you." I saw Clarissa's hands tighten into fists, and I knew my friend wanted to fight for me.

"I know that, theoretically, but it doesn't change how I feel."

"You know I do not give men the benefit of the doubt, but..." Clarissa broke off and turned her knees toward me. I turned back at her movement and caught her stare. "What if she was lying?"

"What do you mean?"

"Something about that woman felt off. I've never gotten an off feeling about Jackson." Clarissa got up and started pacing the living room. "What if she lied about them being engaged. Hell, what if she lied about them even being a couple?"

"Why would someone come all the way out here to Ardor Point and then lie about something like that?"

Clarissa stood still in the middle of the room, looked at the walls that were devoid of any photos of family or friends, other than one of she and I together, and then turned back to me. "Think about it. No one here knows anything about you or where you're from. You could have a whole family you walked away from, and we wouldn't know. You can't say you haven't taken advantage of our more isolated world up here."

When Clarissa turned back to me, there were tears in her eyes.

I jumped up and quickly tied the throw around me to cover up my nakedness, which was a stark reminder of how painfully quick Jackson's departure was. I put my arms around her. "Hey, why are you crying now? It's my heart breaking." She moved out of my arms and turned away, wiping at her eyes with her sleeve. My anxiety rose. *Were those tears because of me? What had I done?*

"I'm sorry. I just realized the truth. I don't actually know you. You entered our world my junior year of high school and were nice enough to give me a job. You trusted me and listened to me. You gave me a safe place to land when my home was a hard place to be. You've become like my big sister, but I know nothing about you." She sobbed, and my heart shattered.

Tears burned the backs of my eyes, and I felt the full weight of the public isolation I'd built here in this place. "Please give me a second to put something else on." Though it was true that I suddenly felt uncomfortable with my lack of clothing, I also needed a moment alone. I walked into the bedroom and closed the door before leaning back against it. Tears ran freely. Rissa was right. I had taken advantage of the isolation and never let anyone know me. I'd wanted to be someone else when I came. The town had afforded me the space and opportunity to integrate myself as a quietly eccentric woman with a mysterious past, and they'd accepted me. I never thought any of it would hurt anyone else.

I exited the room fully clothed a few minutes later with a shoebox. My eyes were swollen from the tears I shed over Clarissa's pain and disappointment, and my throat was tight from simply handling the box in my hand. Clarissa was sitting on the couch rubbing Miel's back while the cat sat quietly on her lap. Neither of them looked up at me. They both meant so much to me that I had to cover my mouth to stifle the sob that threatened to come out with each breath.

"I'll make us some more tea. In the meantime, I want you to see something." I handed the box to Clarissa. There were questions in her eyes when she looked up, but I just shrugged and gave her a tight smile. Miel jumped from her lap and stretched, digging her claws into the rug at my feet. I picked up the mugs and entered the kitchen with Miel at my heels. The cat jumped onto one of the bar stools and meowed for head pats. I grabbed treats from the cabinet as well as teabags and sat waiting for the kettle to boil.

After ten minutes, I placed the hot mugs and some left-over cookies on a tray to carry into the living room. When I pushed open the swinging door, though, I heard Clarissa sobbing. I set the tray on the end table and sat on the floor in front of Clarissa's feet. Thankfully, I was still limber enough to get up and down off the floor easily. Flexibility had always been one of my various partners' favorite things about me. Clarissa looked up at me with puffy, red-rimmed eyes still brimming with tears.

"Hey," I said softly.

"Oh my god, C, I didn't know. I'd have never thought... Shit!"

"Yeah. I never wanted to hurt you or anyone. I just..." I trailed off. Clarissa deserved more than painful photos. She deserved the whole story. "Only one other person in the world knows my whole story. She is my therapist and long-time friend."

Clarissa nodded. "You don't have to relive it."

I shook my head. "You were right, Rissa. I did take advantage of the isolation and the ability to meld into the community without giving too much of my past away. It was exactly what I needed ten years ago. I no longer felt the need to hide for maybe the last five years, but by then I was afraid of how others would judge me if I told them, so I told myself it wasn't necessary. I didn't realize how maintaining that separation also limited the relationships I've been building here. You are like a sister to me. I don't know how I would have survived the quiet of this place for this long without your energy."

Clarissa smiled. I smiled back and pulled the box into my lap. I dug through the photos, stopping occasionally to sigh or wipe a tear from my eye. "How sad is it that thirty-five years of my life fit into a shoebox," I said aloud with a shake of my head. "I moved around a lot as a kid, and I continued that pattern into adulthood. In fact, I think this is the longest I have ever lived in one place. It's hard to collect physical memories when you have to be ready to pack whatever can fit in your car and make moves to the next location." I looked up to see Clarissa staring at me wide-eyed. The young woman had barely left Ardor Point for more than a day at a time.

"Honestly, I loved the nomadic life. It saved me from the pain of many close relationships and provided so many job opportunities. Corporations love people who can pick up and go wherever they're needed and remain objectively focused on the business' needs. I was hardcore and cutthroat."

"No fucking way!" Clarissa's genuine shock made me laugh. She'd only known me to be open and care about my customers. There was a distinct difference between working for a large corporation that cared only for the bottom line and working for myself with the customers directly. I was able to make that distinction, but it made the last few years of my previous life difficult.

"So, being dominant all the time at work often left me depleted and killed my desire to make any decisions in my personal life. To balance it all out, I became a sub."

"A sub?" As worldly as the girl seemed to the people of their town, Clarissa was still quite innocent to many things in the rest of the world.

"Yes, I would go to parties and clubs, and let men, and some women, dominate me sexually. They would tell me what to do, and I'd do it. They would tell me what they wanted to do to me, and I'd let them. All consensual, of course."

"Whoa, that shit happens for real? I thought it was just something made up in a book."

"It happens, and it was what I needed at the time, or at least it was what I thought I needed. Because I had no real family to connect with and little time to build genuine friendships, I struggled to tap into my emotions. I was empty, but I never considered not living, if that makes sense. It was an emptiness that was searching for something." I looked at Clarissa intently, trying to judge her understanding. She nodded.

"I understand that feeling well. You helped me work through it, and I love you for that."

I set the box aside and got up on my knees to hug her. There may have been nearly twenty years difference between us, but I had never felt closer to anyone else. "I'm so glad I was able to help. The search didn't go so well for me because David found me and became the person I poured all of that need into. I stopped going to the parties and clubs. I became his submissive doll at home and his eye candy everywhere else." I pulled a photo from the bottom of the box and showed it to Clarissa.

"Damn! You were hot. Did you dress like this all the time?"

I looked at the photo, memories flooding. I wore a red lingerie set that consisted of a demi-cup bra and lace thong. My hair hung down my back and between my breasts. I had on black and red stilettos that looked like they were covered in flames. The tops of my black thigh-high nylons were laced with red as well. This was the only photo I had saved from the boudoir shoot I had done early in my relationship with David when I still felt sexy.

I laughed. "No, not all the time. At work, I was in power suits that were both strong and sexy. I was there to dominate the men who thought they were running the businesses. I was good at that job, but I hated it." I put the photo back into the bottom of the box. "Anyway, I thought David loved me, but he just loved the control I allowed him to have over me. When we got to the point, I no longer felt sexual gratification from him, he suggested we do some breath play. At first, it was hot."

My thoughts trailed off to the first time he'd held my neck in his hand. He had been taking me from behind. I'd had my hair in pigtails, and he'd pulled them so tightly, my back was bowed. The sex felt so intense, and when he put his hand around to grab my neck, it added to the intensity. The newness of it shortened the experience because we both found our release almost immediately. The second time...

"You saw the photos of the aftermath of the last time. He nearly killed me. My larynx was so bruised, I couldn't talk for weeks. I couldn't work, and I wouldn't leave the house without a scarf. When I didn't wake up, thankfully, he called 911. He didn't wait for them to get there, though, and since I couldn't talk for so long, he had time to go into hiding. It was a little over eight months before I saw him again, and I freaked. I packed up my shit, whatever could fit in my car, and I just drove. I found myself up here in these beautiful mountains. The isolation of Ardor Point when I pulled into Sammy's gas station was so peaceful. I quickly found this house, paid cash out of my savings, and never left."

"I'm glad you stayed," Clarissa said in response. "You are as much a part of this community as I am, and I'm glad that we could be a home for you." I smiled up at her, a single tear streaking down my face. I didn't bother to wipe it away.

It was far after midnight, and Clarissa couldn't hide her yawns. "Let's get some sleep," I offered. She agreed and headed off to the rarely used guest room. I gathered up the tray of cold tea and stale cookies, returned them to the kitchen, and made my own way to bed. I'd deal with everything else tomorrow.

Chapter Sixteen

CAROL

I woke earlier than normal. My eyes were still puffy, and I felt exhausted, but today was a big sales day for the shop, as everyone began their Christmas preparations. I left Clarissa asleep, and, after feeding Miel, headed to the flower shop. I was surprised to see one of the trucks in the parking lot already. Their sign said they weren't opening until 10am, and it was barely 7:45. I wasn't ready to deal with Jackson or the aftermath of last night, so I rushed into the shop and locked the door behind me. I wouldn't unlock it again until we opened at 9:30.

Rather than wear one of my bohemian skirts and loose tees, I opted for a pair of stretchy jeans that contoured perfectly to my curves and a cable knit sweater. The temperature had dropped significantly overnight, and it wasn't supposed to warm up much throughout the day. I knew I had some deliveries to make, and it would likely be busy. I needed warmth and ease of movement.

I organized all the floral arrangements for the deliveries and double-checked the shipment of pine garland that had come in Wednesday before we closed for the day. We had also received a few pots of poinsettias that I'd have Clarissa set up outside when she came in. Poinsettias were our biggest seasonal item, but I wouldn't put in the big order for another week or so. I'd learned over the years that most people here wanted their trees up and decorated before they purchased the traditional flowers.

At 9am, the door chimed, and I heard Clarissa's voice. "I'll be back in a second. Let me check on Carol first." I smiled at her concern. There was no need. I felt good now that I'd had a couple of quiet hours of productive work under my belt. I was thankful for the busyness.

"Hey there, boss lady," Clarissa said from the workroom entrance. I raised a brow at the unexpected title. "You left early this morning. Why didn't you wake me up?"

"You know I never expect you to get here as early as I do. Besides, I kept you awake late enough last night. Thank you, by the way."

Clarissa nodded with a smile. "What's on the agenda for today?"

"We need to set up the displays, pine garland and poinsettias."

"I'm on it," Clarissa said as she turned back toward the front of the shop.

I know you are, I said to myself. For all the negative that could have come out of last night, I was grateful for the lifted weight that was the deepening of my relationship with Clarissa. We each went about our chores preparing for the opening bell, and it was looking to be a busy opening. Every time I carried something out into the shop, I noticed more cars in the parking lot. The guys might want to open at the same time we did to take advantage of the potential customers who were waiting. Regardless of what happened and any awkward conversations to come, I still wished the tree shop well because if they had a good season, I made a healthy cut.

"What in the hell..." Clarissa's voice pierced through to the workshop, and I dropped what I was working on.

"Is everything ok out here," I asked, walking through the double doors. Clarissa was standing at the door staring into the parking lot toward the tents. "Should we open a few minutes early?"

Clarissa quickly turned around and met me halfway to the door. "Everything's fine," she said. "No need to open early. In fact, we might give the guys an extra few minutes and let them take the first group that has arrived."

I scowled, reading something in Clarissa's behavior. "What's going on?"

"There's nothing to worry about. Just go ahead and finish what you were doing, so we can both be out here when we open the door." Clarissa had put on a bright smile, and I almost relented. Then Jackson's voice boomed from outside.

"What the hell are you doing here? You're supposed to be on your way back to California."

Clarissa and I exchanged a look, and the girl covered her face with her hand.

"So, Jackson's unexpected visitor has unexpectedly shown up here this morning. He doesn't sound any happier about it than I am. Let's just stay in here and mind our business."

"I just want to get a look at her," I responded, stepping around Clarissa and heading toward the windows that provide an open view of the lot. There was already a crowd, but one woman stood out as not belonging. She was a tall, thin, platinum blonde and dressed to the nines. She had on a leather pencil skirt with stilettos, and a striped blouse with a large bow at the neck. She could have just walked off a runway in Milan. I remembered the days I used to dress like that, and I imagined the power this woman intended to wield with her outfit in the middle of the small, mountain town. Who, though, was her intended victim?

"There's just something about her I don't like," Clarissa said from my right.

I had known Jackson was not from around here, though he had toned down his dress, but now I realized why I had been so pulled toward him. He reminded me of all I'd given up. He was just a bit nicer, a bit softer, than the men from that world. At least, he seemed to be when he was with me. "So that's the type of woman he likes, huh?" I shook my head. I wouldn't go back, especially not for a man. This beautiful woman could have him.

Jackson had left the tent and was standing in front of the woman. I couldn't hear what they were saying, but neither of them looked happy. There appeared to be a crowd growing around them, and Jackson's team stood at the tent's entrance just watching. Travis stood back behind the others, a worried look on his face. Marc's hands were clenched tight like he might need to jump in and protect his boss.

"Text Marc and ask him to move the crowd. They don't need an audience. The town has enough gossip available without adding to it."

"I'm on it."

They watched as Marc turned to the others and they all spread out to move on the crowd. Travis, however, stayed in place, watching the situation. He was biting his cuticles.

"What in the hell is Travis doing? He should be helping. I'm going to go out and help," Clarissa said, pushing past me.

"Rissa, wait." She didn't listen, just exited the building and began talking to the folks gathered around.

I watched as the opening of the door caught the woman's attention. She looked toward Rissa and then turned her gaze on the shop. Her voice raised loud enough that I could hear her, and the hair prickled at the nape of my neck. *This bitch is itching for a fight.*

"I know that bitch is somewhere around here. I think I deserve to see what you left me for. Homewreckers shouldn't be able to hide."

Jackson responded through gritted teeth, but loud enough that I could hear before the door closed fully. "I didn't leave you for anyone. I left you because of you. Go home, Diane."

"I bet she's in that shop there..." Diane's voice faded as the door closed tightly. She turned and started walking toward the shop.

Oh geez, here we go. I braced myself, but Clarissa and Jackson intercepted Diane. I didn't know whether to be mortified at all the drama coming my way because of their actions or grateful that they stepped in. Either way, the town would be talking about Jackson and me for weeks to come. This would not bode well for the season or my sanity.

"Move out of my way," she screeched at Clarissa. "Let go of me," she yelled when Jackson caught her arm. "Come outside, you backwoods bumpkin! You can't steal my man and not face me!"

I rolled my eyes and took off my apron. I looked in the mirror and patted my hair into place. I wasn't dressed as well as Diane, but I was glad I'd chosen the jeans and sweater combination that hugged my figure.

"What's going on here," came another voice from the parking lot. The crowd separated and let Nick through. I watched on in horror as Jackson's jaw clenched. Leave it to Nick to show up at the worst time for his grandson. "Jackson, unhand that woman. You know better than that, boy." Jackson did as he was told, and Diane immediate made for the door. Clarissa grabbed her and pushed her back. "I repeat, what in the hell is going on here?"

Clarissa shot a glare at the old man, but she didn't let go of Diane. The woman was still howling like a banshee trying to make her way into the shop. I took a deep breath and pushed my way through the door and out into the parking lot to face the madness. Jackson's jaw dropped, as he looked me up and down. Even in this chaotic situation, a ripple of excitement ran down my spine at his response. Nick was also standing in the lot, mere feet away slack-jawed, though if it was at my attire or the entire situation, I couldn't tell. I turned my attention to Diane.

As soon as I had stepped out of the shop, Diane stopped the dramatics and stood with a smile that was more of a sneer. I had met plenty of women, and men, like this. They wanted attention and then would try to play victim to the crowd once they had it. If the woman wasn't beautiful, the crowd standing around would have already tossed her off into the street, but instead they watched to see what would happen next.

"You," Diane said in a tone that was almost a question.

"Me?" I wasn't going to play into these games. "You are on my property causing a commotion and stopping the flow of business. So, I should be the one asking what you want here."

Diane's face turned red. "You know who I am, bitch. You thought you could take my man and not face me about it."

"I'm sorry, do I know you? Have we met? You sound like you know me, and yet you're dumb enough to try and bring the bitch out."

Diane sputtered when Clarissa let her go, but she didn't step any closer. She opened her mouth as if to say something but seemed to think better of it.

"Let's clarify something. If, and that's a huge if, I did what you are accusing me of, you had better check that your man," I gestured with air quotes around the last two words, "made it known that he was taken. Now, I don't know what brought you to Ardor Point or who gave you the audacity to show up at my shop with this nonsense, but I suggest you go back where you came from and where you're wanted."

The woman shrieked but turned on her heel. She slapped Jackson on her way to the car without stopping her stride, and peeled off, stones flying. Everyone standing around lifted their hands to protect themselves from the small rocks that covered the lot. I simply watched the car leave until Clarissa was standing next to me, asking if I was ok.

"I'm fine. She is the type who is all bluster until you step up to her. She wanted an audience to try to make others look bad." I shook my head. "Let's get the shop open, so these people have something else to do beside stand around and gossip." I took one more glance toward Jackson, but he was in an animated conversation with Nick. I wanted to get closer and listen in, but it didn't look good. Instead, I turned my attention to the crowd. "We're open everyone. Sorry for the delay."

Chapter Seventeen
CAROL

The rest of the weekend and the entire following week passed without incident. Nick had turned around and left within the hour of arriving on Friday. He said he had just come to bring the trees they needed to restock, but I wasn't so sure. Jackson's fiancé, or probably ex-fiancé now, had to have found out from Nick where to find him. Ardor Point isn't just somewhere you go looking for someone. I thought about Jackson often, but then I'd push the thoughts from my mind. It wasn't that he brought drama to my doorstep but that he didn't give me any type of warning. I was all about consent and transparency. Still, I found myself watching out the window far too often, even on days like today when the rain was often too heavy to see the other side of the lot.

"You know, you could just go talk to him," Clarissa said from behind me.

I turned toward the boxes of poinsettias I had been unboxing without a response.

"Look, Carol. I know you miss him. I have it from Marc that Jackson misses you too. Both of you are just being so damn stubborn."

"Mind your business, Rissa. There was nothing to miss."

Clarissa snorted and started back to the workshop. Within seconds, though, she returned. "I just need to say one more thing, and then I'll let it go. In the ten years you've been here, I have never seen you so happy. You were smiling every day and laughing all the time. Hell, you even invited people, besides me, to your house for a holiday dinner party. So, tell yourself whatever the hell you have to in order to make it through the day, but don't give me that bullshit that there was nothing to miss." This time, she walked out of the shop door and ran across to the tents, her boots splashing through the puddles left from the last heavy downpour.

I took a deep shuddering breath. I didn't want to think about missing Jackson. He had re-awakened me sexually, and now I was constantly on edge. More than that, I had enjoyed our banter and the way we watched out for each other. There had been many nights this past week that I picked up the phone and had to stop myself from texting him. It wasn't fair that he couldn't have just been fully open with me. We both knew this thing we had was only for a season, so why hide things from each other.

Movement caught my eye, and I looked up to see Clarissa and Marc leaving the tent. They were holding hands under a large umbrella. Before they arrived at the street, Marc pulled her into a passionate kiss. I smiled until I felt someone watching me. Jackson was standing in the opening of the tent. The rain was heavy enough that I could not read his expression, but I had no doubt he was watching me. I wanted to wave, but doubt held my hand. Frustration drove me back to the workroom where I couldn't see him, and hopefully, wouldn't continue to think about him.

Chapter Eighteen

JACKSON

C larissa ran into the tent, dripping water from her hair, mud clinging to her boots. They were all prepping to close, but Marc stopped what he was doing and went to her. I had to smile at the couple. At least one good thing had come out of this crazy season here. I prepared to turn away when something Clarissa said caught my attention.

"Why are they so damn stubborn? They stand at opposite ends of this damn lot and look toward each other but can't be adults and speak. It's maddening. She's all grumpy and mopey, and over here you all get the silent treatment."

I stood a little straighter. I wasn't ignoring the team. We worked together every day. We rode back to the hotel and got dinner together damn near every night when I didn't decide to go to the bar first. Shit, was I isolating myself?

"Hey boss, do you mind if I get out of a here a couple minutes early? I'm going to walk Clarissa home."

I stared at my assistant for a second before his words

processed fully. "In the rain? Why not just take the truck? I'll get a Lyft."

"You sure?"

I nodded and waved him off. I lifted my hand and waved to Clarissa who looked at me sadly before turning away. I could hear the other guys tying everything down and checking the ropes in case the wind picked up in the storm. Rather than going to help them, I followed the couple to the tent's entrance. I wouldn't admit it aloud, but I couldn't deny that Clarissa's words were true. I missed Carol something crazy. I saw a movement inside the shop and turned to see Carol standing in the window. I couldn't see her features because of the rain, but I could picture her just as clearly as if she were standing next to me. Shit, I've got to get her off my mind, I chided myself.

When she moved away from the window, I went back to finish the closing procedures. I sent the other men off for the evening and thought about walking back to the hotel in the rain. I needed to clear my thoughts. After locking up the tent, I noticed Carol's car was still on the street in front of the shop. They had all agreed to park on the street, so customers could get into the lot easily. The lights were still on in the shop as well. She should have gone home by now. I pulled out my phone thinking I would send a text asking if she was ok, but my legs were already making their way toward the door. When I found it still unlocked, I sent up a prayer of thanks.

I opened the door and cringed before the bell even chimed. Her voice came from the back room. "I'm sorry, but we're closed." I turned around and locked the door, so no one else could sneak in on her and walked toward the workroom.

"You're very trusting," I said from outside the swinging doors. "I could have been a serial killer." I didn't need to see her to know that she jumped at the sound of my voice. The crash of boxes was all the tell I needed.

"Dammit, Jackson!"

I pushed through the doors to see her bent over picking up boxes and small adornments she puts on her flower arrangements. Her ass was as glorious as I had remembered, and my fingers itched to touch her. "So, you remember my voice?"

She stood slowly and turned to face me. Her eyes were dark, pupils wide, and my cock lurched at the desire I saw in them. If she took one step toward me, I'd be lost inside her before we could both breathe. Please take that step, I thought to myself.

"No one else is dumb enough to sneak up on me in my own space," she said and took a sultry step toward me.

My mouth opened, as a wave of desire washed over me. "So, I'm dumb now?"

"Yes! You sneak in here after nearly two weeks of radio silence, knowing that I knocked the fuck out of someone with a shovel before. That's not very smart of you." She was within arms' distance now, and I couldn't pry my eyes from hers. "Why are you here, Jackson?" she asked, her voice barely a whisper.

I blinked at the question. Why was I here? What crazy thought pulled me across the lot and into her space like I had any right to be here? "Um, I..."

"You what?"

"I was worried when I saw you were still here this late, and I know Clarissa had already left."

"Is that all? You were worried about me? You could have sent me a text. I haven't blocked your number."

My mouth went dry, and my jeans were uncomfortably tight. I couldn't keep the huskiness out of my voice when I said, "Carol, if you take one more step..."

"You'll what," she said, not missing a step when she came close enough for me to breathe in the scent of her shampoo.

"This," I said, grabbing her hair to pull her head back and crushing my lips to hers. A soft moan left her lips before I invaded her mouth with my tongue. I needed her. No more taking my time or trying to control my desire in favor of hers. Her hands scratching down my back said she wanted this just as much as I did.

I pried my lips from hers, and she whimpered. I trailed kisses down her jaw to her neck, pulling the soft skin between my teeth, and she gasped. I looked behind her at the half-empty worktable and growled. My hands reached down to cup her ass, and I lifted her until she wrapped her legs around my waist. *That's it, baby.* No words were necessary, but I smiled into the curve of her neck at the knowledge that she wanted this as much as me. I carried her to the table and sat her on it. She had on one of her flowing skirts again, and though I loved watching her in the jeans she occasionally put on, I was glad for the easy access.

She was licking up my neck and nipping at my earlobe by the time I reached down to pull the skirt up. She moaned in my ear when I squeezed her upper thighs, and I felt pre-cum seep out of my cock. Fuck, she was going to end this before it started. I needed to take control back. I touched her panties and found them damp already. I groaned and pulled them to the side, so I could slip two fingers inside her.

"Jackson, mmmmm, fuuuuuck."

"That's it, baby, come for me." I moved a little to the side, so I could get better access, and began pumping my fingers in and out of her. She matched my hand with every stroke, and I couldn't wait to be inside of her. My thumb found her swollen clit and made small circles around the nub. Her breath hitched, and I knew she was close. I'd had her there before and was ready for when her walls clamped down on my hand, and she tried to pull her thighs together. I was in the way, though, and didn't let up the onslaught until she laid back on the table, spent.

I pulled my fingers out of her and stuck them in my mouth. "Damn, you taste so good!"

"Jackson."

"Yes, baby."

"Fuck me before something else happens."

I had my pants open and cock out before she could finish the sentence. She sat up and watched me. I stood there and let her eyes see every inch of me. They widened slightly as she took in my size, but then they returned to the lust-filled slits I'd seen earlier. She reached down and ran her hand over the bulb of my head. The touch was delicate and soft. I basked in the feel of her hand on me finally. She trailed kisses along my clavicle as I fought to maintain control of my need for release. I grabbed her wrist and pulled her hand up to kiss it. When she looked at me questioningly, I shook my head.

I pulled a condom out of my wallet and threw the wallet on the ground. I watched her as she watched me roll it until it stretched over the fullness of my cock. Her mouth opened slightly before she bit her bottom lip. The response was so sensual, I couldn't wait anymore, and I reached to pull her hips to the edge of the table. Lining up the tip to her opening, I kissed her. She put her arms around my neck and her hands in my hair. I slid into her with growl. She was so wet and so hot.

"Shit," she said against my mouth, and I smiled.

"Damn, you are perfect, woman."

I slid slowly out of her and then rocked her hips gently against mine, so that I was fully sheathed at the end of each stroke. Her soft moans egged me on, and my pace quickened. She tightened around me, and I nearly lost it. I stopped for a second, but she wasn't ready to let me go and kept rocking her hips, tightening her walls around me.

"Fuck, Carol, this is going to be over too damn soon if you keep doing that."

Carol smiled at me, actually smiled at my need.

"You little minx," I growled. "Put your legs up on my shoulders." My tone left no room for denial. I put my arm around one of her legs and used my thumb to find her clit.

Her eyes opened wide, as I pulled nearly completely out of her while rubbing the nub, still sensitive from her last orgasm.

"Jack…"

I plowed back inside her fast and hard, and she screamed out the rest of my name. I was going to make this worthwhile and began pumping in and out of her hard, our bodies clapping together on each stroke. My thumb continued its swirling at the same time as her moans turned into screams. When she tightened around me, pulsing in her release, I went with her. My cries drowned hers out, and I saw stars.

It was moments before either of us moved and even longer before we said anything. If I hadn't felt myself slipping out of her, I may have stayed that way forever. "Do you have a bathroom back here?" Without a word, she pointed toward the back corner of the workshop behind some shelves. I pulled out and waddled my way through the mess of boxes on the floor, pulling up my pants enough that I wouldn't trip over them.

I closed the bathroom door and stood against it for a minute. There weren't supposed to be feelings involved with this thing. Hell, this wasn't even supposed to be a thing. But it was, and there were. I heard my grandfather's words that afternoon after Diane had left. *Boy, I don't know what you have going on here, but don't let me have to remind you that Carol is my business partner. We've had a good relationship for the past five years. Don't fuck it up with your city slicker bullshit!* Of all the things the man had said to me since I arrived at the tree farm, this one bothered me the most. I had no control over growing up in the city. I didn't decide where my parents, my mother, would bring me or not bring me. Why was the old man pissed off at me? I shook my head from those painful thoughts, cleaned myself up, and splashed some water on my face. "What am I supposed to do now," I asked my reflection in the small mirror over the sink.

I walked back out to the workshop, but Carol was

nowhere to be seen. On the worktable where she had been so beautifully laid out for me, was my wallet and a note.

Please lock the door on your way out.

She'd walked out on me. She hadn't even picked up the boxes I'd scared out of her hands earlier. "Dammit!" I had hoped to talk to her. I had only come over here to talk to her. Damn my lack of self-control where she was concerned. I set about picking up the boxes and stacking them neatly on the table. Grabbing a pen I found near the door, I wrote a quick response. I then placed the note on top of the boxes for her to find in the morning and made my way out of the shop, making sure the door was locked tight before I walked to the hotel.

Chapter Nineteen

CAROL

As soon as I got home, I poured myself a glass of wine. Miel came and sat on my lap on the couch. I didn't bother to put the wine bottle away. Instead, I poured myself a second glass when that one was finished. What had I been thinking egging him on like that? I was grown enough to know what would happen. Hell, I was grown enough to have enjoyed every damn second of it. So why did I just run away like a college student who'd woken in the morning full of regret? There was no regret. I simply couldn't name the feeling I had.

I picked up the phone and text Rachel. I knew it was late for an official call, but the benefit of your best friend being your therapist is that you get after-hours support. I hadn't talked to Rachel in weeks, not since our typical Thanksgiving greetings. I hadn't even mentioned Jackson in that short call. This one was going to be a doozy.

Hey Ray. You busy?

Immediately, my phone rang, and Rachel's voice pierced the silence. "Is everything ok?"

"Yeah, I'm ok, I guess." Rachel's concern made me laugh. "I'm not hurt, I don't think. No, I'm not hurt. I'm confused and need to talk some things out. You got time?"

I began with the day Jackson showed up, and how I was instantly attracted to him. Rachel understood the confusion in that moment since no other man had even piqued my interest in years. It felt good to share these concerns and feelings with someone who truly knew me.

"I told him about David." Rachel gasped. "Ok, I didn't tell him everything. The only person who has heard that full story is Clarissa. I love that girl. She's like the little sister I never had."

"I know she's grown to be very important to you," Rachel said softly.

She knew all about Clarissa and understood what had drawn me to the girl. I'd easily offered her a job her junior year of high school and was so glad when she decided to stay on. Though I'd have rather Rissa had gone away to college to see what life was like away from her family, I was thrilled to have her working year-round at the shop. Our friendship helped keep me connected to the town, so the urge to pack up and return to the city wasn't so great.

"He's a city boy, Ray. Everything about him speaks of the city, except for the way he talks with people rather than at them."

"So, what brought him there to your mountain hideaway," Rachel asked. I told her about Nick and what Clarissa had heard from her boyfriend, Marc. "Sounds like you feel bad for him."

"No, I don't just feel sorry for him. This isn't like bringing home a lost animal. I was attracted to him before I knew how Nick was treating him and the randomness of the team." I told her about the incident with Freddy, and I almost thought she would jump through the phone in concern for me. Then I shared how I had saved Jackson's life with a shovel. That part of the story relieved the tension, and we both laughed. It was much easier to laugh about it now. In the moment, I had been terrified.

"It seems like a lot has happened in the short time you've known each other," Rachel said. I couldn't tell whether she was amused or critical.

"Yeah, we've known each other about five weeks now, give or take, and so much has happened." I told Rachel about all the times we almost had sex. I knew that much of the tension Jackson and I held for each other was because of how close we had gotten on so many occasions. I wasn't naive to think it was more than that, but I couldn't help that spark of hope that maybe there was more. "The last time, on Thanksgiving, his fiancé showed up."

"His what did what?" Rachel was incredulous. "What in the hell is wrong with men? Why is it so hard for them to just be honest and tell us what is what? Do they really think there aren't women who want the same things they do, sex and entertainment? Geez!"

I sat silently while Rachel ranted about good-for-nothing men for a good five minutes more. She wasn't wrong, and so many of the things she said applied to most of the men I dated in my twenties. Somehow, though, those criticisms didn't seem to fit Jackson, no matter how upset I had been with him. "I don't know, Ray. His response when that woman showed up at the shop and tried to pick a fight with me made me want to believe him more. He had tried to protect me and my business. Of course, I went out and told her to stop her dramatics, but he seemed genuinely upset that I was upset."

I explained how we had stayed away from each other for nearly two weeks. Neither one of us had spoken about it nor made it a conscious mutual decision. It was just easy to get caught up in the busyness of the season. I didn't, however, share with her how I'd watch for him through the window, or how I'd look at the texts we had sent each other leading up to Thanksgiving. Across those weeks, his name was still the one I cried out when I got myself off thinking about our intimate times together. Thankfully, she didn't ask about any of that.

"Then he walked into my shop today, and I damn near jumped his bones, Ray. No, seriously. As soon as I heard his voice from outside my workshop, my entire body was on fire. He easily reciprocated my desire, and the next thing I knew, I was on the worktable, and he was pounding in and out of me. It was the sexiest and most powerful I've felt in years." I paused for a minute, and Rachel began spewing questions, asking for details.

"What? After all the anxiety and angst, you just fucked it out on your worktable? Ok, note to self that if you ever finally invite me to visit, I will not touch that table. Also, was it good? Did he last? What's he working with?"

Therapist Rachel had taken a break, and this was my best friend. "He was everything I needed, Ray. Even though he'd never gotten off any of the times we'd been intimate, and I knew he was straining, he still made sure I had two orgasms first. And I didn't need any kinks to get there." Rachel went silent. She knew that I had struggled with finishing without any extra help from outside sensations. "I needed nothing extra, just him."

"I'm so happy for you. You needed that release. So how did you feel afterward?" She elongated the 'so' in such a way I knew she was almost afraid to ask the question. The answer wasn't much easier.

"I ran, Ray. That's what I did. I wrote him a note to lock up behind himself. I grabbed my purse, and I left him there in the bathroom to clean up the mess. I feel like such an asshole." The guilt of leaving is why I called her to begin with. I wanted to apologize to him, but I didn't know how. I had to talk to someone about it. "It was probably the best sex of my life, and I ran. What the hell is wrong with me," I asked, nearly in tears. An hour later, I was in tears for another reason.

"Hey, don't beat yourself up, but really think about what it is you want from this," Rachel said. "Normally, I would not give prescriptive advice to my clients, so take this from your best friend. Give him a chance. Let him knock the rest of the cobwebs away. If nothing else comes of it, at least you will have felt alive again for a while. You've spent so many years worrying about what might happen that you never just let things happen. You're freaking out because he makes you feel. Not only has he awoken your emotions, but he's renewed your connection to your own body. That can be scary considering where you came from when you stopped yourself from feeling completely."

I had no argument. She wasn't wrong. I worried about far too many what ifs, like what if that chick really was his fiancé. Or, what if he had every intention of going back to California in a few weeks? What if he never wanted to come back again because of Nick? If I gave myself permission to see where this would go, would I be able to then let him go? We ended the conversation with all these questions floating around through my head.

Chapter Twenty

CAROL

Head woozy from the near-full bottle of wine I'd finished off, I dragged myself to bed. It was going to be a long night, and I was going to regret it all in the morning. My head no sooner hit the pillow than I was asleep, thoughts of Jackson floating through my mind. I felt like I was in my favorite children's movie 'Twas the Night Before Christmas, the one with the mice. 'While visions of sugarplums danced through their heads.' Only thing was, my sugarplum was a perfectly made man who touched me in all the right ways. Our dance was one of tongues and limbs.

A loud rattle outside my bedroom interrupted my dreams. What in the hell had that damn cat knocked over? "Miel, go lay down somewhere!" Miel's meow from beside my head scared me more than the loud noise, and I jumped to a seated position. My head was still a bit loopy, so I couldn't have been asleep for long. "Who the hell is in my house," I said to the purring kitten next to me. I slid into my slippers that, thankfully, were right next to the bed and padded over to the closet where I kept a bat. Ready to swing, I opened the bedroom door and looked out into the living room.

On the floor was the box of photos I still hadn't put away from when I told Clarissa about my past. I walked out of the room and knelt to retrieve the contents. A photo from when I was 15, alone by a lake, was facing up at me. It was one of the only photos of me where I hadn't plastered on a fake smile. The lake was frozen, and we had gone out there to choose our Christmas tree and ice skate as a family. When I got out of the car, my parents drove off with my siblings. This was their punishment for me refusing to follow some arbitrary rule they had made up and changed on a whim. They took this photo of me from the car as they watched me from behind thick bushes. As soon as the photo had been developed, and they showed it to me, I decided to pack my bags and leave home. I wasn't yet 16 when I spent my first Christmas at a halfway house in another state.

The room lit, and I turned to see an incorporeal figure looking at me with sad eyes. She was young, maybe 20, maybe younger. It was hard to tell by the way she flickered in and out of view. I rubbed my eyes, unsure what I was seeing.

"Who, no, what are you?"

She pointed toward the photo, and I shook my head. "I don't want to think about the past." I hadn't thought about this photo in years, and I'd be damned if a drunken stupor would make me start.

"You need to remember," the ethereal voice said, sounding almost sympathetic.

"I don't need any reminders of being alone. I'm alone right now. I still know what that feels like. I don't need to think of my family abandoning me."

The figure blinked, and I was no longer in my house. Instead, we were standing in the middle of an over-decorated home. *What the hell?* The Christmas tree lights were bright and blinking in time to the carols that were playing in the background. A child sat at the end of a long dining-room table. His dark hair was cropped short, and he was dressed in suit pants, a button-down shirt, and a bowtie. He was drawing something. "What is he drawing?" The specter gestured for me to look.

On the paper was a forest of pine trees. There was a pickup truck with a tree sticking up off the bed. He had drawn a little boy that looked a lot like him along with an older man and woman. They were all smiling. He had drawn a house with smoke coming from the chimney in the background. It was such a cozy drawing that did not match the sad look on the little boy's face. Then arguing filtered in from the other room.

"We are not going to that gods-forsaken mountain, Patrick!" The woman's words gave Carol pause, and she looked down at the drawing and the little boy again. It couldn't be.

"Hush, Natalie. Jackson doesn't need to hear us arguing." I placed a hand over my mouth in case anyone should hear my gasp.

"Let him hear. Let him know how his father is trying to force us to travel to the middle of nowhere at Christmas when we have parties and exciting events planned here."

"Those are my parents, Natalie! Jackson loves going to see his grandparents, and we already said we were going."

"No, you said we were going. I did not, would not, say that, and Jackson is never going back there again. He is made for much better things than a tree farm. He is going to own companies and command respect."

"Natalie, be reasonable."

"I don't know what I ever saw in you. I thought you were ambitious. I thought you wanted more than that small-town-nowhere life."

"Oh my god, is that what he dealt with as a child?" I

turned to the ghost, and her sad eyes told me all I needed to know. Tears traveled down my cheeks. She flickered, and we were in a cemetery. It took me a moment to get my bearings. "Where? Why are we here?" She said nothing but pointed beyond a small hill.

I walked past a large willow, its floating branches not touching my face as we passed through. "Wait, am I dead?" My breaths came faster, and my heartbeat increased. She shook her head. "A dream then?"

"Memories," she said. Why would she be showing me Jackson's memories?

Again, angry voices permeated the air around me.

"How dare you show your face here," came a man's shouts. I recognized that voice. Nick?

"He was my husband, you old coot. He was my son's father. We have more right to be here than you do. You held him back from greatness with this tree farm legacy!"

I barely held back a gasp, as I found little Jackson standing stoically behind his mother. His face held no emotion, and he didn't look at his grandfather. He was a few years older than in the last memory. Dream? It had to be a dream.

"You stole my son from me, and now you keep his son from us too. You are a witch!"

Jackson's mother laughed, a dark, terrible cackle that prickled the hair at my nape. "I've seen enough," I said. The ghost flickered again, and we were in a hospital waiting room. I recognized this place, and when I looked around, I saw Rachel's parents. The doctor came through the door.

"Rachel and the baby are both fine. There were some complications, but they both made it out fine. It will be another hour or so before you will be able to see either of them." Tears stung my eyes, as I remembered the worry and the relief. I looked around at her family, and I remembered how jealous I had felt in that moment knowing that I wouldn't have any family waiting for me should I somehow be in the hospital. I turned away from the scene. The ghost put her hand on my shoulder. It was supposed to be such a happy time, but I had been anything but happy.

In the next moment, we were in a bar, and I saw myself sitting with David at a high-top table. We had just met, and all my emotions flooded. I watched myself smile and flirt with him. In a flash, we were at his apartment. The two of us were in the bed. I had faked my orgasm, and we lay apart, not touching. He was asleep, and I stared at the ceiling. Another flash, and we were at dinner for our anniversary.

"I have something special for you to try. I think you'll like it. We haven't done anything like this before. Think of it as an early Christmas present." My body tensed, and I closed my eyes against the memories of what would happen next.

"I don't need to see anymore. I know what's going to happen here. Why are you showing me this."

She flickered, and we were back in my living room. Miel wrapped her body around my feet and purred loudly. The ghost looked at me, her eyes empathetic. Who did she remind me of? I couldn't think, but I know I recognized her.

"You have always struggled to recognize the purpose of life. You stopped enjoying the individual moments and tried to force forever on what was only for now. Then you let it ruin you for the future." *What the hell?*

I had no words, and she faded from sight. I returned the pictures to the box and carried the box to my bed. I fumbled through the memories, allowing the tears to flow. I knew it was late and I would truly regret tonight's decisions when my alarm rang in the morning, but I couldn't stop. I looked at the last family photo my parents had made of us all. It was for the Christmas cards my mother sent out to our extended family and friends. We looked like the perfect Hallmark family. I wonder what the card said the year that I left.

I thought back to the visions of young Jackson, and my heart broke for him. There was no way those could have been his memories. Somehow, my drunken subconscious wanted me to feel sorry for him. Still, I was even more angry at Nick now for the way he treated Jackson when all his inner child wanted was to come back to where he was happy. And I'm not sure I would be able to meet his mother without having words with her. How could she be so cruel? I fell back to sleep with the image of his drawing in my head.

Chapter Twenty-One
CAROL

I t was near impossible to make it through the day and not think about my visions from the night before. It had to be a dream, but it all seemed so vivid. I could still hear the voices, and I found myself near tears numerous times. More than once, Clarissa walked up to me helping a customer and asked if I was okay.

"I'm just tired," I'd said. Though it was true, she eyed me suspiciously.

Apparently, Jackson had a rough night as well. He didn't roll into the lot until after noon, and he looked completely disheveled. I wanted to go to him, but when he didn't look toward the shop, I thought better of it. We were so busy with a line down the walkway when I got to the shop this morning that I didn't make it into the back workshop until after the lunch rush cleared, somewhere around 2pm.

I had forgotten about the boxes I had dropped all over the floor and prepared myself to clean up the mess before Clarissa noticed. I looked over my shoulder to see her working with customers at the front of the shop. I pushed through the swinging doors and stopped short. All the boxes were stacked neatly on the worktable. Had Clarissa come back here without me noticing? I walked closer and saw a folded slip of paper on top of the stack.

I'm sorry.

Jackson had cleaned up our mess. Dammit, why did he have to be so considerate? I looked at his words again, and tears escaped my closed eyes. He had nothing to apologize for. I was wrong for leaving. The door chimed again, and I heard lots of voices. Wiping my eyes, I refolded the paper and slipped it into my apron pocket. I would eventually figure out what to say to him.

We had our busiest day ever. Sales were higher than they'd been any of the previous seasons. Clarissa looked wiped out, so I sent her home. When I closed up and walked outside, the tree shop was dark. Both trucks were gone from the street. Oh well, I was too tired to argue anyway. I made my way home, after a detour at the bank, and climbed into my bed fully clothed. I immediately fell back asleep.

Christmas music and bright lights woke me. "What in the hell?" I covered my eyes from the brightness and then realization hit. I was home alone. I sprang to a seated position and opened my eyes. I still had to cover them until the glare cleared. In front of me was an apparition that looked like Santa Claus dressed as Friar Tuck. He also reminded me of someone, but much like last night's ghost, I couldn't quite figure out who. The ghost laughed, and his cheeks bulged out. Had he been drinking? "What in the hell?" I asked again.

"Get up and ready. We have places to be," he said, his voice as bright as his smile.

I flopped back on the bed and covered my eyes. If this were a dream, I refused to participate. "Do I have to? What more could you possibly show me that I didn't see yesterday?"

I heard his robe swishing before I felt his cold hand touch my foot. In a flash, we were out of my bedroom, and I was lying on the floor of an elevator going up. I jumped to my feet and brushed myself off. For as friendly as this dude sounded, he was inconsiderate as hell, and I felt my temper flare. I was prepared to tell him about himself when the elevator bell rang that we had reached the penthouse. The doors opened, and someone entered the elevator, walking through the friar. I blinked, my heart beating erratically. *Please let this be a dream.* I followed him into the crowded foyer, doing my best not to touch anyone. "Where are we?" I whispered.

He laughed again, and pointed in the direction of the far wall, near the floor-to-ceiling windows. I looked around then. Cocktail dresses and tuxedos must have been on the invitations because everyone was impeccably dressed. I saw the Christmas decorations, an obviously professional job, and sighed. "I am terribly underdressed for a penthouse Christmas party," I mused.

"They can't see you anyway," the ghost retorted. I rolled my eyes at him, trying not to show my apprehension. Finally, I looked in the direction he had pointed. Standing across the room was Diane, the bitch who had brought her overly dramatic bullshit to my shop. I walked through the crowd, making sure not to touch anyone. I didn't know what I'd do if someone just walked through me like they had the ghost.

The closer I got, the clearer her shrill voice became. "He refused to come home. Can you believe that?" I knew she was talking about Jackson, and my hackles rose. She was talking with a red-headed woman who was turned away from me. I almost walked around them, so I could see her face, but the voice pierced my heart.

"Yes, I can believe that. Ungrateful, just like his father. I hope the bastard rots. I will take care of my son. He will be back soon." I wanted to scream. I wanted to slap both women. How could they be so callous?

"That's fine," Diane said. "In the meantime, I'm going to have some fun. Let me know when my fiancé gets his shit together." She smiled and turned to grab the hands of the couple standing directly behind her. "Come my lovelies. I need something this party isn't giving." The lascivious grins on the faces of the man and woman turned my stomach.

I turned to the ghost, "Please tell me I was never that crass and callous, and fucking entitled."

"I am not the one for memories. I live in the now. Shall we?"

He grabbed my shoulder, and we flashed to a smaller, more intimate gathering. I didn't recognize the location, though I could tell through the windows that we were in some high rise. "Another party?" He simply smiled and pointed toward the living room area. A woman sat on the sofa, and a man leaned over her, whispering something in her ear. I couldn't hear them, so I started walking closer. The woman said something, and the man stood to walk around in front of her. I saw his face and gasped. Christopher. I looked at the woman, moving myself into a better position to see her face, and tears sprang to my eyes. Rachel looked so beautiful.

Chris squatted until he was face-to-face with her and nuzzled her nose with his. "Don't be sad, my love. She will come one of these years. We will just keep inviting her." She shook her head.

"I want you to be right, Chris, but I know Carol. She keeps herself distant purposely. I told you we talked the other day, and she's at the point of breaking her own heart again."

I wiped a tear from my eye. Is that what I was doing? Chris grabbed Ray's hands and helped her up. I gasped and a sob escaped my throat. She was pregnant again, very pregnant. I looked at the ghost. "Is this now, this year?" How could she be pregnant and me not know it. *Oh my god*. I was the worst friend ever.

The ghost neared and reached out his hand. "Can we just stay another few minutes, please?" His smile faltered. "This is my dream after all." Still, when he touched my shoulder, we flashed to a snow-covered mountainside. In front of me was a cabin, much like the one young Jackson had in his drawing. I recognized it immediately as Nick's home, though I'd never been there. I looked down at my feet. Although I only had on socks, and we were standing in more than a foot of snow, my feet were neither wet nor cold.

Friar Claus, as my brain wanted to call him, led me to a window on the side of the cabin. I could see Nick standing in the kitchen doorway talking to an older woman who looked so much like Jackson, my breath caught. I never saw Jackson's father, but I can only imagine that Jackson must look like his twin. Even in her sixties, his grandmother was beautiful. Her face contorted in anger, and I watched tears roll down her cheek.

"He's so close, Nick! I want to see him."

"You don't need your heart broken again, Mae." Nick stood in the doorway with his arms folded. He looked just as implacable as he had when talking to Nick in the lot the day Diane was there.

"My heart hasn't been whole since we put Patrick in the ground and saw Jackson for the last time. I need to see him." I struggled to hold in a sob threatening to escape. My heart was breaking for her.

"I can't do it, Mae. I can barely look at him. He refused to come see us for nearly 30 years." His voice cracked at the last part, but he wasn't budging.

"But he came now. He came now, and he's taking whatever punishment you've dealt him." Mae walked to her husband and took his hands.

"I can't," Nick said, an obvious hitch in his voice.

I found myself hoping he'd break for Jackson's sake. I wished I could show Nick that drawing little Jackson had made. I wished I could warn him about Diane and Natalie's plans for Jackson. I stood at that window, close enough that my breath should have been creating a fog effect, but it wasn't. I heard the ghost's swishing robes behind me and prepared myself for the next painful vision. When I opened my eyes, though, we were back in my bedroom, Miel nuzzling my hand for me to pet her. I looked up to see the ghost fading away. He looked much more tired than he had when he'd arrived.

I, too, was exhausted. I looked at the clock, and it was already 2:30am. I needed some sleep, but I couldn't stop replaying the scenes the ghost had shown me. What was I supposed to do with this information? If I told anyone, they'd think I was crazy. I couldn't fully say I wasn't crazy. My brain was fucking with me. I stripped out of yesterday's clothes and fell into a fitful sleep, hoping it was all a dream.

Chapter Twenty-Two
CAROL

I woke to the sound of a bell tolling. At least it sounded like the clang of a bell, one of those large brass church bells. There was no church near enough to my house for me to hear that.

The clanging happened again, and I opened my eyes to the dark room. I got out of the bed and grabbed a long t-shirt to cover my naked body. One of these days I'd learn better than to sleep alone in the nude. Heading toward the bedroom door, I grabbed my trusty bat. I had never used it on anyone before, but I did feel safer with it in my hands. The door to my room opened easily, and the living room was empty, other than Miel sleeping on the back of the couch. Oddly, she didn't move when I walked through the room. What was going on?

Approaching the kitchen door, I tightened my grip on the bat. Thankfully, it was a swinging door, so I didn't have to release the metal weapon to turn a knob. The kitchen glowed with an eerie green light, and I sighed, a tremor going up my back.

"I don't need any more heartbreaking stories or crazy warnings. I'm already exhausted." I said before I even saw the ghost standing in the middle of the kitchen. He was tall, nearly seven feet and fully hooded, a huge bell hung around his neck. I could not see his face, though I knew it to be a him, but the skin of his neck was pure white, as was his hand when he lifted it to gesture me forward. "What are you," I asked, shrinking back from the hand that reached for me. Rather than grab my shoulder like the other ghosts had, he held his hand in front of me and waited for me to touch his sleeve.

I did not have time to register the thinness of his arm, or the smell of damp earth that wafted from his robe when my hand touched it, before we were whisked away to a dark alley. Heavy bass emanated from behind the metal door in front of us. A couple of young girls, overly made up and wearing dresses that barely covered their asses, walked in front of us like we weren't there. The clicking of their high heels stopped before they banged on the door. How'd they know to come to this door in this alley? I watched, expecting a tall, burly bouncer to open the door. Instead, a thin, nerdy kid, maybe Clarissa's age, probably younger, stepped onto the landing. He looked at them, and his lips twisted into a sneer.

"Back again?"

"Look, we have IDs," the taller of the girls said.

The kid rolled his eyes. "Those IDs are faker than your knock off Jimmy Choo's. Come back when you're 25."

"You're not even 25, Parker," the shorter girl said.

The smile he turned on them made me feel bad for the girls. He may have been young, but they were out of their league. As soon as he opened his mouth to retort, the ghost lifted a hand and pointed at the door.

"You want me to go in there?" What in the hell could I possibly need to see in there, I thought. When he didn't lower his hand, I snuck around the door and entered the... *What in the hell was this place*? I looked around, but there were walls and hallways in all directions. A noise from above drew my attention to scaffolds crisscrossing through the air. People were walking across them and staring down into the space beyond the walls. What was happening here? I looked over my shoulder at the ghost. "Is this a..." Before I could finish the question, he pointed down the dimly lit hall on our right. At the end of the hall were a set of stairs that led to the scaffolds.

When I stepped up onto the landing, the muscles of my legs tightened, and sweat beads formed on my forehead. The people looked like specters floating through the air in the dark. The blaring music shook the floor beneath me, and I reached out a hand to steady myself on the wall. I had no desire to step out on those planks. My hooded companion turned to the right and led me down a narrow passage along the wall. I took in a deep breath and let it out slowly.

At the end of the passageway was another landing with a low wall overlooking the open space below, an observation deck of sorts. The thumping music still pulsed beneath my feet, but the ghost's robes barely rippled, though he stood near the low wall. I approached slowly, grasping onto the beam atop the wall before looking over the edge.

I gasped. Jackson was in the room below. He was seated on a chair in the corner of the room, head lolled back as if asleep, but he was not asleep. His eyes were open. In front of him, a woman was getting railed by two men in full-coverage masks. Her platinum hair clung to her face and the man she was riding. Diane. I shook with anger. *What was he doing here with her? What game was she playing with him?* As if on cue, the sound of the music faded, and I could hear her moans. Against my will, my vagina clenched. I'd always been aroused by the sound of another woman's passionate enjoyment. Diane raised her head toward Jackson.

"Look at me, Jackson. Knowing you're watching me get off gets me off."

Bile rose in my throat, and any arousal died with her words.

"You came back to me. Remember that. Your little fling sent you home packing, and now we will do things my way. Come put your dick in my mouth."

When Jackson stood, defeat written in his every move, I turned away, tears running down my cheeks. Was he that broken? Did I break him further by rejecting him too? I grabbed the ghost's sleeve and closed my eyes, more afraid of the scene below than the specter next to me. Thankfully, we were somewhere else when I reopened them.

I recognized the house. The other ghost had brought me here. This was Rachel's house. I rushed up the stairs, praying someone would open the door before I got there. Maybe she'd had the new baby. The house was silent. Though daylight was dwindling, no lights shown in the windows.

A cab pulled up to the curb, and Christopher climbed out of the backseat. He held out his hand, but the person who stepped out of the cab was but a shadow of the Rachel I had known. This woman was pale and required his arm to guide her up the stairs.

"Come now, Rachel, you need to talk to someone. If not to me, then call Carol."

Rachel gave him a wan smile that barely covered the melancholy in her eyes. A sob got lodged in my throat. What had happened to my vivacious friend?

"I haven't talked to her in over a year, not since she sent that California dude packing. She hasn't called, text, or responded to anything on social media. She shut down again, and I can't depend on her."

Christopher's eyes were sad, and my heart broke for him. He lived for her, and she was obviously hurting. I tried to reach for her hand while Chris fumbled for the house key, but my hands passed right through hers. I jumped back as if burned.

"I just want to go to bed...alone, please," Rachel said. Chris' head dropped, and his shoulders drooped. He unlocked the door and silently ushered her through.

The sound of thunder shook the leaves from the nearby trees while tears streamed down my face. "Are these visions of things destined to happen or things that might happen?" The ghost did not respond, instead lifting his arm for me to grab once again. "I don't want to see anymore," I said, knowing it did not matter. He would give me three visions, just as the others had. I took a deep breath and touched his robe.

This time, we flashed into a hospital room. I looked at the patient in the bed. His eyes were the only thing visible beyond the respirator and gauze that wrapped all the way around his head. *Who was this?* I walked around to the end of the bed where the patient chart is usually placed. Nicholas Branch. My breath caught. *Nick?* Voices echoed from the hall.

"Sir, sir, you can't just go in there."

"He's my grandfather!"

Through the window, I saw Jackson trying to get around a nurse and orderly. Though his hair was disheveled, as if he had run his hands through it numerous times, he was dressed impeccably. His black suit was tailored to fit his body perfectly, and his shoes gleamed under the harsh hospital lights. The anguish on his face stole my breath, and I wanted to go to him. The ghost stepped into my path, keeping me in place.

"We need to see some identification," the nurse said. "What is your name, sir?"

"My name is Jackson Branch. A friend who works for him called and told me about the accident. I jumped on the first flight I could get."

The nurse took the card Jackson offered her and wrote his name on her clipboard. "Are you his next of kin?"

"Yes," he answered after a few second, and his voice

cracked. He took a deep breath. "My grandmother died a couple years ago."

Handing back the ID, the nurse explained that Nick had an accident while driving a load of trees off the mountain. He did not make one of the curves and slid off the side. Thankfully, there was a slope, and the truck drove down the side rather than flipping, but it didn't stop until it hit a large tree. I looked back at the man I had known for the past seven years and tried to bite back the tears for what felt like the hundredth time tonight. When the nurse finished retelling of Nick's numerous injuries, she stepped out of the way, and Jackson entered the room.

He pulled the chair to the side of the bed and sat down with his head in his hands. After several minutes, he grabbed for Nick's hand. "How is your hand so warm when you let your heart get so cold?"

I gasped at the venom in his voice. That did not sound like my Jackson. *My Jackson? Since when had I claimed him as mine?* A sudden thought entered my mind. I was being tortured with these spectral visits because I wouldn't give him a chance. Maybe these were visions that would only happen if I didn't change my ways. I could only hope because I hated what I was seeing.

Jackson dropped Nick's hand and began pacing the side of the room along the bed. "I came," he said and paused, looking again at his grandfather. "I'm here because I had hoped we could finally reconcile, finally talk through whatever grudge you held against me, but you're not really here, are you? Your body is here, but you're not here." He let out a sob and wiped his hand across his eyes. "Dammit, why did you hate me so much? All I had were fond memories of my childhood summers here. All I wanted for years was to come back, but you abandoned me when my father died. You forgot about me." The tears were flowing freely now, and he did nothing to stop them. "Instead, you blamed me. I was a kid! I needed love. I needed protection. I needed you!" Slamming the chair back against the wall, he flopped into it. "I needed you," he whispered into the sudden silence.

A loud beeping came from the heart monitor, drawing my attention from Jackson. Then a loud alarm sounded. Jackson was back on his feet. Nurses and doctors came running down the hall, filing into the room. I made to follow Jackson when they ushered him out of the door, but the ghost stood in my way. "Please, let me go to him! I need to go," I pled. "He needs me!" The ghost reached out his two hand and enveloped me in his robes. Everything went black, as I fought against the cloth.

"Let me go, he needs me!" The robes twisted around, holding my arms against my body until I couldn't move freely. Still, I squirmed, yelling for the specter to let me go. I had to get to Jackson. I had to let him know he wasn't alone. This was not something anyone should have to go through alone.

Suddenly, I was on my side, falling through the air. "Oof." I hit the ground with a thud. My eyes flew open, and my face was shrouded in white. *What in the hell? Where was I? Did the God of Death bury me?* I began fighting against the cloth in earnest again when suddenly it slipped, allowing fresh air to brush against my face. I turned in the direction of the air and saw my closet. The door was slightly open on its slider, and my bat was standing against the wall. "What the hell?" I asked aloud, stopping my squirming.

I looked more closely at my bindings. The tag from my sheets hung down in front of my face. I let out a long breath. It was just a dream. As I worked to unwrap myself, Miel jumped on top of me. With my newly freed hand, I pet her absently, listening to her purr. The raw turmoil from the lingering visions was fading, but a deep sadness settled into my chest, heavier than my cat. It took a few minutes, but I was finally able to get up from the floor. I threw the sheets in a twisted heap onto the bed and then, bone-weary, fell back onto it myself.

Chapter Twenty-Three
JACKSON

At 9am, Clarissa came running over to the tents. "Has anyone seen Carol this morning?"

"Her car wasn't here when I arrived," I said, coming from behind our makeshift counter where we kept the lockbox and card reader.

"And you didn't think that unusual?"

"Of course I did, but it's not like she answers to me. Hell, I haven't even talked to her in days."

Clarissa's eyes went wide. "I thought you two had made up. Anyway, that doesn't matter. She's not here, it's opening time, and she's not answering her phone." Her voice had raised in pitch and loudness. She followed the statement with a meaningful look that I took as a call to action.

"Ok, I'm going to check on her." In fact, I was already checking my pockets for my keys and walking toward the open tent flaps. "Marc, you're in charge."

"I'm on it, boss."

Before I started the truck, I watched Clarissa walk across the lot to the shop and turn the sign to open. I smiled at the girl. Her work ethic and loyalty, not to mention friendship, were commendable. She was right, though, Carol would not just not show up for work. Something had to be wrong. I turned the key and peeled out of my spot on the street.

I was approaching Carol's street when a thought hit me. What if she had met someone else? I didn't want to intrude on her. As soon as I had the thought, I dismissed it as a lie. I definitely wanted to intrude. The very idea made my nostrils flare and my muscles tense. She wasn't like that. She wasn't Diane, and the idea of someone else touching her triggered my possessiveness. No, something had to be wrong. If it was a man, she was in trouble and needed help. Adrenalin pumping at my jumbled thoughts, I took the turn a little too fast and my tires spun out, the truck lifting on the one corner before I could get it straightened out.

I pulled into her driveway and parked next to her car. Good, she's home, I thought, as I took the stairs to her door two at a time. I knocked twice and waited. No response. I tried to look through the front window, but I saw nothing moving. The room was still in shadows. I knocked again, multiple times. Her cat, Miel, jumped up in the window, and the hair rose on my arms. *Shit!*

"Carol," I called through the door. I pounded with the side of my fist. "Carol, are you in there? Are you alright?" My heart was pounding, and I considered busting through the door. Did she have a back door? Which end of the house was her bedroom? Why hadn't I asked for a damn tour of the house on Thanksgiving? I pounded my fist against the door again "Carol!" I dragged out the syllables, and finally, I saw movement in the living room.

Seconds later, Carol opened the door. I quickly swept her into my arms and hugged her tightly. "You're alright. Thank goodness, you're alright!"

"Jackson," she said in a muffled whisper. "I can't breathe."

I released my grip and brought my hands up to her face. Her eyes were drooped, and there were dark circles under them. She looked exhausted. I ran my hands down her arms trying to push away the urge to grasp her tightly again. When she didn't move but also said nothing, I lifted her chin. Her eyes fluttered open, and I felt her sway a bit.

"Hey, are you alright? You look exhausted."

"I'm just so tired," she said quietly and swayed again, her eyes half closing.

I reached my arm down behind her legs and picked her up, walking back in the direction she had come from when she opened the door. The far door was open, and I saw a large, disheveled bed. From the way she sunk into my arms and closed her eyes immediately, she must have spent the night tossing and turning. I lay her down with her head on the pillow and covered her with the sheet. Her comforter was half on the floor at the other side of the King-size bed. When I stepped away to grab it, she turned to look at me.

"You're not leaving, are you?"

"No, but I am going to call Clarissa and let her know that you won't be in."

She sat up quickly. "What time is it?"

I hurried back to her side of the bed, leaving the comforter where it was, and knelt on the floor. "It doesn't matter." I smoothed the hair back from her face. "You are in no condition to run the shop today."

She turned panicked eyes to me and made to get off the bed. "What do you mean? I can't not open! This is the busiest time of the year."

I put my hands on her shoulders to keep her from getting up. "Carol, the shop opened almost an hour ago. Clarissa has it under control, and Marc is right across the lot if she needs anything."

"I can't leave Clarissa alone all day in the middle of the

season. That's not fair. It's my responsibility." There were tears in her eyes.

I pulled my cell from my back pocket and called Marc. "Hey, can you go next door and put Clarissa on the phone? I don't have the number of the shop saved in my phone." She looked up at me, and I gave her a soft smile. The weary sadness and guilt in her eyes nearly broke me, but there was no way she was going in today. "Hey, do you need Carol to come in today?" I emphasized the word need, hoping she'd get my meaning, and I put the phone on speaker.

"So long as she is ok, I think it is a brilliant idea for her to take a day off. She never takes any time. Thanks for checking on her."

Carol opened her mouth to say something, and I disconnected the call. She tried to grab my phone, and I put it in my back pocket. When she reached for hers on the bedside table, I put it in my other pocket. She turned angry eyes on me and pouted. I nearly chuckled, but I stopped myself. She needed rest.

"Be a brat if you want to, and when you're feeling better, I will show you how brats get handled," I said with a wink before fluffing her pillow. "Now, put your pretty head on this pillow and go back to sleep." She didn't stop pouting, but she finally acquiesced. I smiled down at her and grabbed the comforter.

"You're really not leaving," she asked.

"No, ma'am. You're going to let me take care of you. I don't know what is going on, but you're obviously not feeling quite yourself today."

She gave me a wan smile and didn't argue. Her eyes closed, and within seconds, her breaths evened out, telling me she was asleep. Marc had text me Clarissa's cell number, so I called to let her know what was really going on. She was not surprised Carol had tried to come in once she realized the time and was grateful I was here to make sure she stayed put.

Chapter Twenty-Four

CAROL

The smell of bacon woke me from my dream. Thankfully, this had been a normal, peaceful dream. Of course, Jackson was in it, but there was no worry or angst. We just sat on the couch watching a movie and throwing popcorn at each other. Why in the hell was I smelling bacon? It was too cold for my neighbors to have their grill going. Padded footsteps came through the living room, and I froze. Could I get to my bat before they got to the room? Would they hear me and come faster if I moved? *Shit!*

I pushed off the covers and put one foot on the floor, when the doorknob turned. I looked for my phone, but it wasn't on the bedside table where I always put it at night. Did I leave it in the car? I was so tired last night. The door pushed open, and Miel jumped on the bed. I breathed a sigh of relief. Silly cat had figured out how to open the door. I nuzzled him, burying my nose in his fur.

"You're up," came a man's voice, and I screamed.

Miel, startled at my cry, tried to jump out of my arms and left welts in my skin with her claws. I screamed again, this time in surprised pain.

"Hey, hey, it's just me."

"Jackson?" I looked up. "What are you doing here?"

He smiled at me, his beautiful teeth sparkling from between those kissable lips of his.

"You really don't remember letting me in hours ago?"

I thought really hard, but I could not recall much of anything since I came home last night. I shook my head. What was wrong with me? I knew I was tired from lack of sleep the past two nights, but still. Tears burned the back of my eyes, but I swallowed them down.

"I was coming to wake you up to eat. It's already after three, and you haven't eaten anything, I'm guessing, since yesterday." He sat on the bed in front of me and reached over to grab a tray from the other side of the bed. There was a plate with scrambled eggs, bacon, and toast, a glass of orange juice, and a single mum he must have pulled from the bouquet I had on the island in the kitchen. The gesture was so sweet, a rogue tear ran down my cheek and I quickly wiped it away before looking at his face.

"You cook?" The words slipped out before I could stop them. "Sorry, my mouth works faster than my brain."

Jackson laughed, a full belly laugh, and I couldn't help but to laugh with him. "No, I let Miel handle lunch."

"Wait, did you say lunch? Did you say it was after 3...pm?"

Jackson's smile fell, and he looked at me squarely. "Eat before the food is completely cold, and then we can talk about it." His tone bore no argument, and I had none to give. I couldn't believe I had slept through the day. I pulled my feet back onto the bed and Jackson placed the tray on my lap.

"This really is super sweet of you. Thank you," I said between bites. The eggs were fluffy, cheesy goodness, and the bacon was cooked perfectly with crunchy edges and enough chewiness to not be brittle. I moaned in delight, and Jackson shifted in front of me, adjusting his seated position. A wicked thrill ran up my back. The food was just what I needed to gain some energy, and my body had an idea on how to expend it. I went to take a sip of the orange juice and wound up chugging it down in one go.

Without a word, Jackson grabbed the glass off the tray and left the room. He came back with two glasses in his hand, one with water, and one with juice. He clinked them together before placing them both on the tray with a smile. I reached up and grabbed the front of his shirt, pulling him down for a kiss. I'd meant it as a light kiss to say thank you, but the moment his lips touched mine, my body ignited. I gasped at the intensity of my desire, and his tongue invaded my mouth, twirling around mine in the most sensual dance. He moaned and I put my arms around his neck to pull him closer. He slid the tray from between us, somehow not spilling either of the drinks, and placed it on the bedside table.

"Are you sure about this," he asked. "You weren't feeling well this morning, and I don't want to exhaust you more."

I didn't answer his ludicrous question. Instead, I kissed him again and pulled him down on top of me. Before he could situate himself, I caught his momentum and pushed him onto his back, rolling with him. His hands rubbed up and down my thighs, while I straddled his waist. His erection pressed through his jeans, teasing me through my panties. I rubbed myself forward and backward against his body, and his breathing hitched. The friction of his hardness through our clothes was driving me crazy. *Dammit, why was he still dressed?* When he said my name in a breathy whisper, I stopped and slid down until my knees were between his.

He watched me in silence. I pulled up his shirt until I could see the small trail of hair that led from his belly button to below his waistband. I kissed where the trail began and ran my tongue down as far as I could reach with his pants on. His eyes were glued to me, and that gaze made me even wetter. I opened his fly and watched his cock try to escape the confines of his underwear. Using the heel of my hand, I rubbed up his full length until my fingers could encircle the head, and then I freed it to my touch. It stood at attention for me, and I had to squeeze my legs closed at the sensation pulsing between them. Damn, every inch of this man turned me on.

I watched Jackson's face as I grasped his shaft in my hand and stroked it. He hissed and laid his head back on the pillow, bottom lip between his teeth. A smile crossed my lips while I waited for him to look back down at me. He didn't leave me waiting for long, and as soon as our eyes locked, I leaned down and took the head of his cock into my mouth. I made circles around that bulb with my tongue until he moaned, and then I slowly worked my way down until I had sheathed him entirely. His mouth opened more at every inch I took, and his breathing got ragged.

"Mmm baby, that's nice," he managed to croak out.

I tightened my lips as I slid up off him. "You liked that?" He nodded, and I smiled, well, more of a smirk because he hadn't seen anything yet. Every time we had been intimate, he had made sure that I was fully pleased, and it was his turn to reap the reward. I grabbed him in my hand again and pulled up toward his belly button. Still maintaining eye contact, I made circles with my tongue on his balls, drawing each one into my mouth. His eyes closed in ecstasy, and my smile grew. My tongue wasn't done though. It slowly made its way up the shaft until I, once again, had the head in my mouth. Knowing he was enjoying my control, I wanted to see how he'd respond to my abandon.

Within seconds, his hand was on the top of my head, moving with each quick and deep stroke. His moans were more frequent and louder. It took no time before his hips were bucking off the bed and his fingers were digging into the sheets. I'm sure if I had looked down, his toes would have been curling. When I pulled him out and slapped the head against my tongue a few times, he grabbed the shaft and turned it away.

"Whoa," he said, out of breath. "I don't want to finish yet."

I looked up at him and bit my lower lip. "What do you want then?"

He sat up, put his hand under my arms and pulled me into him for a kiss that made my toes curl. Next thing I knew, my t-shirt was off, I was on my back, and his tongue was on my clit. This wasn't the tender, attentive service he had previously provided. The way he licked and sucked was primal, and I came from the sheer power of it all, but he didn't stop. He lifted my hips off the ground and fucked me with his tongue. Folding me in half, he repeated the ministrations on my asshole, and I almost came again.

"Fuck, Jackson. I need you in me."

He gave me a smirk and patted his back pockets. "My wallet is out in the truck. You'll have to make do with my mouth and my hands."

I returned his smirk and reached into the drawer of the bedside table, pulling out a box of condoms with a wink. He laughed, grabbed the box and flipped me onto my stomach. I tried to roll back, and he slapped my ass. The sting both surprised me and sent jolts of excitement up my body.

"Stay where I put you," he said, rubbing the spot on my ass he had just slapped.

He climbed off the bed and pulled me onto my knees. I heard the stretch of fabric and guessed he was getting undressed. I tried to look back at him, and he slapped the other cheek. I bit my lip and moaned.

"Didn't I say to stay where and how I put you?"

"Yes, sir."

"Spread yourself open for me."

His commanding voice had me dripping. Who would have

known he had it in him. He was always so sweet and accommodating, putting up with my wishy-washy bullshit. But here, in my bed, he took control, and I let him. Curving my back, I put my arms around the outside of my legs and pulled my cheeks and lips apart, my fingers splayed to make sure he had access to it all. The crinkle of a condom wrapper had me smiling in anticipation. Instead of entering me, though, he rubbed the head of his cock up and down from my hood to my ass. A groan slipped from my throat each time he teased my hole. I was already so wet from sucking his dick that I needed him inside me.

"Don't let go," he said. I felt the absence of his warmth before my brain acknowledged he had moved away from me.

"Jackson?"

"I'm just admiring the view."

"What the hell?"

Two slaps in rapid succession hit each of my cheeks. I yelped at the sting and nearly pulled my hands up to rub the assaulted skin, but he grabbed my hands, holding them in place. Then he kissed both of my ass cheeks with his soft lips. He kissed his way between my cheeks and down to my clit before his tongue assaulted the sensitive nub. I moaned and pressed back into his face, ensuring he didn't lose contact. He let his tongue follow the path his dick had taken and paid careful attention to my asshole, sending tingles up my spine.

"Mmmm," I moaned.

He chuckled against my ass and replaced his tongue with one of his thumbs. I tensed for a second, but his other thumb reached down and rubbed my clit, washing away any uncertainty I'd had. It had been years since I'd done any ass play, and I'd almost forgotten how to relax sufficiently. Jackson knew what he was doing, though, and I let him do it. He pushed his thumb inside me slowly until it was beyond the tight sphincter. He had sufficiently lubricated the area with his tongue, and my moans grew strong with each stroke. Then, he filled me completed, stretching my walls with his cock in the same way his thumb had stretched its way inside too. The dueling sensations were almost too much, and every nerve ending in my body was activated.

"Don't stop. Please." I would have begged at that point.

His strokes deepened, his balls slapping up against my clit on every hit.

"Fuck, Jackson. I'm gonna come."

He gripped my hair and pulled back, sending me over the precipice until I was falling into the waves of my release. His pace quickened, and my moans punctuated every stroke. "Yes, yes, yes, yes." My eyes rolled back, and I lost track of time. I have no idea how long it took before Jackson followed me into oblivion, but I was hyper aware of the emptiness when he pulled out of both holes.

"You did well," he said, and I smiled, deeply satisfied.

He walked into the bathroom and turned on the shower. I closed my eyes and fell instantly asleep.

Chapter Twenty-Five

CAROL

My alarm rang at 5am, and I quickly shut it off. My muscles groaned at the sudden movement, and I closed my eyes against the unexpected soreness. I jumped at the shifting next to me in the bed until I saw a head of dark waves. Memories from yesterday flooded through my consciousness. The sweetness of his breakfast for dinner and the intensity of his worry for me when he first arrived. The passionate control he took while he worked my body last night. Heat pooled between my thighs as I remembered the way he watched my tongue and mouth work on his cock. Even in his pleasure, he made sure I got what I needed from the experience. I closed my eyes against the sudden emotions. He was by far the most selfless man I'd ever known. He shifted again, and I opened my eyes only to find myself reflected in his deep brown ones.

"How did you sleep," he asked, the sexiness of his gruff morning voice taking me back to those earlier thoughts.

I bit my lip and trailed my eyes to his mouth and then over his torso. When my vision settled on the sheet sitting right below his belly button, his cock twitched making me smile. I shifted my legs in response to the tingling at their center.

"Ma'am."

"Hmmm?"

"My eyes are up here."

"So they are," I said, returning his gaze, "and they are beautiful. Blame your incredibly sexy morning voice for my, um, distraction."

He lifted his arm and put it around me, pulling me closer to his chest. "Oh really," he whispered into my ear before trailing a stream of warm breath down my neck. I nodded against the side of his face, as he then followed his breath with a trail of kisses.

"Mmmm." My fingers made circles around his nipple until the tiny nub stiffened. I had always been fascinated by man nipples and the different ways men react when you give them a little attention. I pulled away from his kisses and licked at it, pulling it into my mouth. He hissed and dug his fingers into my back. It was his turn to moan.

I went to shift myself closer for better leverage, and he reached down, pulling my leg over to straddle him in one smooth movement. He didn't need to say anything, as I began giving both of his nipples attention while rubbing my heated core against the length of his erection. In moments, we were both moaning in rhythm. He put his hands in my hair and pulled me up for a passionate kiss, morning breath be damned. I felt myself dripping on his cock, my arousal growing with each movement of my hips. He must have felt it too because he grabbed my hips and changed the direction from front to back rocking to small circles. His head was grinding against my clit, and I sucked my breath in through my teeth. When I came, it was in soft ripples of pleasure that left me panting.

"We need to go to work today," he said, as my eyes drifted closed, and my head rested on his chest. "C'mon, as much as I would enjoy another day in bed with you, Clarissa might kill us both if we leave her alone two days in a row during the busiest week of the season."

"Fine," I said with a pout. "Maybe we should bring donuts for everyone as a peace offering for yesterday."

He smiled and pushed me off him. I watched his tight ass walk toward the bathroom before getting myself out of the bed to do my morning routine. I was in desperate need of a shower and a toothbrush. I let Jackson drive us in rather than take two cars. We picked up pastries at the best little pasteleria in the county on our way into town. Two blocks from the shop, he pulled over to the curb and turned to look at me.

"Hey, before we get back to business as usual, I need to know something." A knot formed in my throat, but I said nothing, letting him continue. "The fact we're riding into work together makes it seem like you will invite me back over tonight." I smiled at him when he paused. I had a feeling of where he was going, but since he didn't ask a question yet, I waited. "I guess what I'm trying to say is..." He took a deep breath and blew it out.

"Every time we've been intimate, something has happened, and I've pulled away. You're worried that as soon as I walk away from you and into the shop, things will change again. Am I right?"

He nodded, and the concerned look on his face reminded me of young Jackson with his drawing listening to his parents argue over whether he'd ever make it back to the tree farm. I had to stifle a sob and bite back the tears stinging the backs of my eyes. It was my turn to take a deep breath.

"Look, I admit that an uncertain future makes me uncomfortable, but I am willing to see where this goes if you are. I am choosing you, Jackson Branch."

He reached out and grabbed my hand, pulling it to his lips. There was so much emotion in his eyes that I wasn't sure he would be able to say anything. Jackson was so strong in so many ways and, like me, broken in so many other ways. Finally, he smiled.

"There are so many things I want to say, that I want to tell you. I have never met anyone like you, Carol. You are so compassionate and giving, so strong and yet soft at the same time. You've been hurt, badly, and yet you're not hardened against others. I can only hope to be worthy of the trust I know it is difficult for you to give."

His words brought on the tears I'd been working so desperately to hold back. He cupped my cheek in his hand and used his thumb to wipe away the stream streaking down my face. He turned back toward the steering wheel and pulled back into the street. When we got to the shop, he refused to drop me off at the curb, instead pulling all the way up into the lot in front of the shop door.

"Jackson, if you don't back this truck up and park it on the street before the hordes of last-minute tree shoppers show up," I teased. "Seriously, park out there." I pointed out of the back window, and he laughed. Finally, he put the pickup in reverse and when he shut the truck off, he pulled me to him for a kiss. "Stop that, or we won't be working today after all." We both laughed and got out of the truck. He grabbed the box of donuts for his crew, and I grabbed the small bag that held my and Clarissa's favorites. We walked up the parking lot hand-in-hand. He kissed my cheek and then walked off into the tent where his guys were watching from the shadows. They were clapping before he entered the flaps.

My greeting was less congratulatory. Clarissa first admonished me for making her worry, after giving me a tight hug, of course. Then she chided me for leaving her alone the whole day. She complained about Mrs. Jensen and her barrage of questions for the gossip mongers. "The old biddy came in talking about how she noticed that you and Jackson were both taking the same day off," she recounted with an air of disdain that had me laughing aloud.

"I love you, Rissa," I said, hugging her again before making my way to the workroom to put my apron on for the day.

Chapter Twenty-Six
JACKSON

The stream of customers was never ending from the moment we opened until after the lunch rush. Did no one in this town work during the day? I had hoped to have a moment to check on Carol and make sure she wasn't exhausting herself, but I never got a chance to leave the tent. As soon as things slowed down, though, my mind wandered back to last night and how enthusiastically she had accepted me and submitted to my demands. At that thought, my pants tightened uncomfortably. I picked up my phone to send her a quick text, and there was already one from her.

> Would it be wrong to take a couple days off the last weekend of the season?

I crashed into the shop, startling Clarissa who was near the door with a customer.

"She's in the back, crazy man!"

"Sorry," I said absently, already halfway down the aisle.

I walked through the swinging doors, and there she was. Her back was to me, but she appeared healthy and whole. I opened my mouth to speak, but she turned.

"Rissa, help me with..."

A small, startled gasp escaped, as the huge poinsettia bouquet slipped from her hands. Thankfully, I was close enough to catch it before it hit the ground. She might have killed me had I not.

"Why is it you always have something in your hands when I walk in here?"

"Why is it you always walk in here like a damn ghost? I need to put taps on your shoes."

A smile quivered along my lips, and I was grateful for the size of the bouquet. There was no way I was going to be able to control my facial expressions when she looked so indignant. It made me want to sneak back here on her all the time. Not sure that would bode well for our budding relationship, though. Wait, were we in a relationship? Between yesterday and this morning, it sure felt like one. Did she want a relationship, with me? Yes, she said she was choosing me. Though my heart burst and my stomach did flip-flops at her words, I still wasn't sure exactly what she meant.

"Where would you like this," I asked to distract my wayward thoughts.

"It goes out on the counter. Mrs. Jensen is picking it up this afternoon."

"The gossip-train conductor?"

"The one and only," she said with a chuckle.

I turned and nearly plowed Clarissa down.

"Watch where you're going with that thing," she screeched.

I apologized again and made my way out to the counter. I had no sooner set it down when I saw Mrs. Jensen getting out of her car. I scurried back into the workroom to hide out.

Carol didn't need her spreading any more tales. She'd have to live with it all if I left town. That thought washed over me like ice water. I didn't want to leave. Yes, I had come here to reunite with my grandparents, and that had gone to shit, but I had no desire to return to California. I had no desire to leave Carol. Fuck, this season was ending far too quickly.

Someone cleared their throat, and I looked up to see Carol and Clarissa looking at me quizzically. Had I said those last thoughts out loud?

"Mrs. Jensen is on her way inside," I said before they could ask me anything.

"I'm on it," Clarissa said and went to leave.

"Holler if you need backup," Carol said to her retreating back.

Clarissa didn't bother to respond or to turn around, and Carol crooked her finger at me to come out of sight of the doorway. At least I thought that was the reason, until she grabbed a hold of my shirt. She pulled me forward with it, and her lips locked onto mine. Wrapping my hands around her back, I pulled her in close, molding her body to mine. She let out a sigh, and my tongue penetrated her open mouth. My hands were in her hair, and her hands were pulling my shirt out of my jeans. The loud ding of the cash register reminded me where we were, and I reluctantly pulled my lips from hers.

"If we don't stop, I'm going to have you calling my name on top of this worktable again. That will really give Mrs. Jensen something to say."

Carol sobered at that last part, and she tucked the back of my shirt in with a whimper. Leaning down next to her ear, I promised to finish this when we got back to the house this evening. Thankfully, we were no longer staying open late, so we could grab dinner and then head back home for dessert.

"You didn't respond to my text," she said, when she finally stepped out of my arms. She turned to pull some flowers out of their buckets and put them on the worktable.

"That's what brought me over here in a hurry. I thought maybe you had exhausted yourself and needed to go home. You don't look and certainly didn't just act exhausted."

She chuckled and went back to work arranging the flowers. "No, I was talking about maybe Friday and Saturday. I have not taken any days off during the season since I started the business. I've not seen my best friend, or her baby, who is no longer a baby, in years. I know she thinks I'm hiding away up here in the mountains."

I repressed a groan. We had so little time left before the season ended, and I had to make a final decision about whether I was leaving or not. "Oh, that sounds like a great idea. You have definitely earned some time off." I tried to make my voice match the smile I wasn't feeling.

"They have a Christmas party on the last Friday before Christmas every year. If I'm being honest with you, maybe I have been hiding. I've been pretty bah humbug about Christmas for more years than I care to count."

Her tone had changed, and I reached to pull her back to me. "The holidays haven't been easy for me either, so I get it."

She turned in my arms, looking straight into my eyes, like she was trying to verify my words, or maybe look for something deeper. It was hard to tell. Finally, she asked if I'd go with her to her best friend's party.

"Unless you can't take off or don't want to go," she quickly amended. "I don't want to make you uncomfortable, and I don't want you to feel obligated." She had a panicked look in her eyes, and her words started coming out faster. I wanted to hug her tight to try and relax the emotion, but I needed her to see my face when I responded.

"I would love to go."

Chapter Twenty-Seven
CAROL

I worked the rest of the week, not only to make sure everything was ready for Clarissa to run the shop alone, but also to put some surprises in place. It was hard, and I was ready to choke a couple of people by the time Friday came, not the least of which Jackson. Every time, I picked up the phone to make plans, he would walk in. It was like he had a sixth sense that told me I was up to something he wasn't going to like. At least, I hoped it would turn into something that would make him truly happy, but he wouldn't like the plan if he knew.

Thursday, I had to tell him I was making an out-of-town delivery and that he could not go with me. I nearly changed my mind at the sad look on his face, but I said I needed him to make sure all the last-minute preparations were in place for both shops. Christmas was on Sunday, so Clarissa and his team would essentially be closing shop for the season alone. Clarissa had some experience with how I shut down the season, but his team did not, this being their first season with the tree farm. He relented, and I put the final pieces of my plan into play.

Jackson had spent every night since Sunday at my house, so before going home to pack, we cleaned out his hotel room. There was no reason for the farm to continue paying for it when he wasn't there, and he wouldn't be back before the season ended. The other guys would be leaving for home Saturday night after closing, so they could spend the holiday with their families. Everyone except Marc. He had finally gotten up the nerve to meet Clarissa's mom, and that went so well, she invited him to Christmas morning. Then the two lovebirds would head out to Marc's family's holiday celebration, and I couldn't be happier for them.

We set out on our road trip at 8am, Friday morning. It would take us six hours to get to Scottsvale where we'd grab a hotel and get ready. Jackson had talked about us leaving later and getting ready first, but who wants to be driving long distances in party wear. We were going to spend the night anyway, so there was no reason to cut our time short. Besides, he had never been to Scottsvale, so there were some things I wanted to show him in the daylight, like where I had worked and the high-rise I lived in before moving to Ardor Point. Thankfully, the weather held out nicely with just a sprinkling of flurries throughout our ride through the mountain passes.

We checked into the hotel around 4pm, and the party wasn't starting until 7.

"I'm going to jump in the shower," I said, stripping my clothes almost as soon as we entered the room.

Having carried everything into the room, Jackson's back was to me. He turned around at my statement and smiled. I slowed my movements, holding his gaze. I had already removed my pants, socks, and shoes. I slowly pulled my shirt over my head and let it fall to the floor. I turned away from him and noticed the giant mirror on the wall behind me. It gave him a perfect view of my front and back from where he had sat on the armchair by the windows. I caught his gaze in the mirror and unclasped my bra, letting the straps slide off my shoulders until I pulled the cups off my breasts. My nipples were already hard under his stare, and heat pooled between my legs.

"Would you like to join me," I asked over my shoulder.

I shrugged as nonchalantly as possible when he shook his head no, trying to hide my surprise. It was hard not to pout under the strength of my arousal. Then, he crooked his finger at me in the mirror, beckoning me to the other side of the room.

"That's not the way to the shower," I said.

"No, but it is the way to get what you need."

I stood in front of him, bare of everything except my panties. They didn't offer much cover from his gaze, though, as they were sheer and barely covered my fluffy vulva. Still, his eyes drunk me in and turned me on with their smolder. Without a word, he slipped his shoes off, and unbuttoned his pants. I smiled. When he lifted up to slide them off of his hips, his cock stood at attention. My mouth watered.

He grabbed the throw pillow from behind his back and put it on the floor between his legs. He didn't have to say a word. I knelt on the pillow and took him in my hands, working the full length between the two. He leaned his head back against the chair and moaned. When he looked back at me, he grabbed my hands in his and pulled them away.

"Just your mouth," he said with a growl. If my panties hadn't already been wet, they were then.

I complied, as he held my hands on either of the chair's arms, while I worked my mouth down the fullness of his shaft. I shook my head, pulling him deep into my throat. He moaned and fisted his hands in my hair, holding me in place until tears sprouted from my eyes. I came up for air and immediately deep throated his cock again. I loved the way he responded.

"Mmmmm Carol. If you keep that up, I won't last to take care of your needs."

Maybe he thought that would make me stop, but all it did was egg me on. I wanted to let him have control when he took it, but damn if I didn't feel powerful when he lost control. I reduced the depth of my sucking and sped up my movements. His moans were low and regular.

"Shit, baby, stop."

I pulled him out of my mouth and look up into his eyes. He picked me up from the floor and put me on his lap to straddle him in the chair. It took a second to get into the right position, but then I was able to lift up and he slid himself right into me.

"Damn, you're so wet."

I started grinding against him, lifting myself to feel his length slide in and out of my heat. This man had me so ready all the time no extra lube was necessary. I couldn't get the right leverage I wanted in this narrow chair, so I got up and turned around. At first, he started to protest, until I reached between my legs, and grabbed him to put him back inside me. Then I could rock my hips freely, feet on the floor between his legs. Every rocking movement had him hitting my spot, and I was getting so close to cumming.

He must have read my mind because he reached around and started rubbing my clit. The pressure in my vagina increased until I was buzzing with the need to finish.

"Jackson, shit, I'm gonna cum."

"Do it," he whispered in my ear, and the response was immediate. I cried out, as my walls pulsed around his cock. He continued rubbing my swollen clit until I came down from the high and began working my hips again.

"Did you get what you needed?"

"Yes," I said, my voice hoarse. Now, I needed some water.

"Good girl. Now go get in the shower. We'll save the rest for tonight."

I turned to look at him. He slapped my ass and lifted me off his cock, which continued to stand at attention covered in my release.

"Are you sure?"

"Oh yes. I like the idea of you owing me when we get back. I may remind you of it throughout the night."

His words made my pussy tingle anew, but I followed his directions and showered. He came in as I was finishing and kissed me silly. He still wouldn't let me touch him, though. When we left for the party, my panties were already wet with his promise of what was to come later tonight. I was just as excited for Jackson as I was to see my best friend.

The night was everything I could have wished for. Jackson and Christopher got along exceedingly well, and Rachel forgave me for all the years I had been missing. I never told her I was only six hours away. Instead, I pretended like I was in a completely different mountain range in a different time zone. She was angry at first but understood my need to start anew and step away from everything and everyone. I didn't get to see the ten year old who had nearly killed her all those years ago, but I was there for the pregnancy announcement, and I couldn't wait to be in this baby's life consistently. They would know who Auntie Carol was. I wouldn't even consider the last ghost's premonition right now. Things could change. The fact that I was here for the announcement with Jackson standing by my side was proof that things could change.

Jackson stayed true to his words about reminding me regularly that he was taking what he wanted that night. He'd whispered it in my ear numerous times and even sent quick text messages about it when we were in separate rooms. He started collecting on that promise on the way back to the hotel when he pulled up my dress and had me turn in my seat to masturbate while he drove. He told me when to rub my clit and when to finger myself.

"You will not cum until I say," he demanded when my eyes rolled back.

In the hotel parking lot, he grabbed my hand and sucked my fingers dry, making my breath catch. The elevator proved to be another point of arousal. He pulled me against him until my mons was grinding against his hardness. And when he kissed me, he pulled the back of my dress up, so anyone who might be waiting when we got off would see my thong. When he finally laid me on the bed and sucked on my clit, I nearly broke his rule. It was so hard to control the need for release that he had built since the afternoon.

"You taste so fucking good," he said, coming up for air.

He slipped two fingers inside of me and then turned his hand around, so he could put his thumb in my ass. I gasped and clamped down on his hand.

"Fuck, Jackson..."

"Not yet, beautiful. Hold out a few more minutes. Those pulsating walls will be my gift once I'm inside of you."

"I don't know if I can..."

"You will." His tone held my arguments at bay, and I bit my lip, whimpering in the strain, while his hand worked in and out of my holes. "You like that, don't you?"

"Yes," I whispered, my breath catching with every stroke. "Jackson, please."

He leaned up and kissed me, his fingers continuing to bring me to the brink. Just when I was about to topple over, he pulled them out, and a tear leaked from my eye. He rolled me over and pulled my hips upward. Without warning, he slammed his cock into my pussy. I let loose a guttural scream of ecstasy when he filled me completely. He pulled out and repeated the action. This time, he worked shorter strokes in and out, grasping my hips, so I didn't go too far as he pushed in. Without warning, he pushed his thumb back in my ass and began pounding into my pussy. I cried out over and over, as the momentum pushed me.

"Now, let me feel you," he said. Within seconds, we were both falling over the edge. He let loose a deep moan, my name falling off his lips. My legs trembled, and with a scream of release, I came all over his dick. I fell forward in exhaustion, and he lay on top of me unmoving. "Time for another shower," he said in my ear before climbing off and pulling me up to walk in front of him to the bathroom.

Chapter Twenty-Eight

JACKSON

Spending the weekend with Carol and meeting her friends solidified what I already knew. There was no way I was letting this woman out of my life. If I needed to, I'd help her run the business or start my own since there were no large corporations near Ardor Point. I would work something out, even if I had to keep working for the tree farm until I figured out another means of income. I'm not sure my grandfather would be happy about that or not, but his opinion no longer mattered to me. The only person who mattered was Carol. She stirred next to me, and I rolled over to kiss her on the forehead.

"Merry Christmas, Ms. Bah Humbug."

She yawned and smiled. "I don't feel so humbug this year, thank you very much." She cupped my face and kissed me. I pulled her close and tried to deepen the kiss, but she pulled away. "I have to get things ready."

"Ready for what? Me, you, and this bed, sounds like the perfect holiday."

She laughed and jumped out of the bed before I could grab her. "We're having company for dinner, silly."

Company? According to Clarissa, my team on Thanksgiving was the first company she'd ever had here at the house in the ten years she'd owned it. What was she doing? Of course, I wasn't complaining. She looked happy, and I'd do whatever it took to keep her that way. Maybe she had talked Clarissa and Marc into coming back to town after they went to his family's celebration.

I got up, made the bed, and jumped in the shower. Miel was sitting in the doorway when I shut the water off. Rarely did I get a glimpse of Carol's cat. She didn't seem to like strangers. "Hello," I said, reaching down to pet between her ears. She meowed at me and left the room. I couldn't help but laugh.

By the time I was dressed and made it out to the kitchen, Carol was face first in the oven, basting what looked like a medium-sized turkey. There was a full plate of bacon and eggs on the counter in front of a half-finished plate of the same. I sat down and put a strip of bacon in my mouth. I guess I was hungrier than I thought, as I set about eating the eggs and toast that accompanied it. I was drinking the glass of O.J. when she stood up and closed the oven.

"There you are," she said with a smile. "Any chance I could get you to set up the tree? Usually, it would already be up because Clarissa would have been here hounding me about it."

I looked at her suspiciously. "Who is coming to dinner, babe?"

"You'll see," she said and kissed my nose on her way into the pantry.

I don't know that I liked that answer, but rather than address something I couldn't change, I asked where the tree was. She claimed it, and all its accoutrement, were out in the shed. She didn't warn me that I would have to dig through the shed, which was more like a detached garage filled to the brim with stuff. I couldn't even come up with a better word than stuff because it was stuffed. Thank goodness, the tree was near the front, and the box of decorations was big and red, making it easy to find. I carried everything into the living room and started unboxing the items. It was obvious Christmas had never been her happy time because everything was thrown into the box without any consideration for preserving items from getting broken or ensuring the lights would still work the next year. Yet, she kept a tree and decorations ready for Clarissa to come over. She really was an enigma.

She jumped in the shower around 4pm once all the food was ready. Our guests were scheduled to arrive before 6, and I could tell she was becoming more nervous as the time got closer. Her answer to my questions got shorter, and her breaths came faster. She ran around the house, straightening things that already looked great. Finally, I cornered her in the kitchen.

"Who is coming that you are about to drive yourself into a panic attack for?"

She stopped and looked up at me, tears rimming her eyes. I wrapped my arms around her.

"Talk to me."

"I don't want you to be upset. I want this to be a great day and everything to work out. Please don't be mad at me."

"Mad at you?"

I had barely gotten the question out when there was a knock on the door. I looked down at her, and she wiped a tear from her eye. I looked back at her before opening the door, and she was wringing her hands so tightly, her knuckles were white. A pit formed in my stomach, as I turned the knob.

A voice I had never expected to hear again said my name,

and my knees went weak. "Grandma?" If my grandfather hadn't been standing behind her looking just as uncertain as I felt, I might not have recognized the white-haired woman in front of me. Last I had seen her, she was in her early 50s with head full of dark curls, similar to mine. Her smile was the same, though, and when she opened her arms to me, I walked into them without a word. She held onto me for so long, Carol walked behind me to open the door wider, so Nick could enter the house.

"It is good to see you, Carol."

"You too, Santa," I heard her say.

She was right. He was Santa and had delivered the best gift. My grandmother released me from the hug, but she immediately grabbed my hands like I might disappear if she didn't maintain the connection. I smiled and invited her to sit on the couch.

"Yes, please, Nick and Mae, have a seat." Carol said. "Wouldyalike somethingtuh drink?"

She raced through the words, and I quickly took over. "We have wine, beer, water, soda, and tea."

They made their requests, red wine for her and a beer for him. Carol exited the room like it was on fire, leaving me alone with my grandparents.

"You look so much like my Patrick," my grandmother said, putting her palms on either side of my face. "Doesn't he look just like his father, Nick?"

Nick merely nodded, clearly uncomfortable. I would not let him ruin this for me. I turned my full attention back on the beautiful woman in front of me.

"I'm so glad you're here," I said to her, and I meant it.

"I'm just sorry it took so long," she responded in kind, glancing at Nick from the corner of her eye. "You must catch me up on your life and what you've been doing since you've been here in Ardor Point. I also must know about you and that lovely woman in the kitchen."

My smile widened at the mention of Carol, but before I could say anything, she came through the door with four drinks on a tray. I rose to grab the tray from her before her nerves had it toppling. I whispered my gratitude in her ear when I was close enough, hoping that would assuage some of her worry until I could properly thank her for whatever it was she did to make this happen.

"Jackson," Nick said, rising from the chair and grabbing his beer from the tray, "Can I speak with you outside, please."

I looked toward my grandmother, and she gave me a small smile and a shrug. That was not exactly the encouragement I was hoping for, but I couldn't just leave him outside by himself. I sighed, grabbed my own beer because I would probably need it, and went to meet my fate. Nick was halfway down the driveway by the time I caught up to him.

"You always had a way of finding me whenever I left the house," he said once I was within earshot. "I used to try and sneak out the back door, and you'd come running around from the front." He paused his musings and looked at me. "Even back then, I knew it could all end any day and didn't want to get too close. Your mother always hated it here. She was miserable and tried to make everyone else miserable. Still, it hurt when you never returned. Mostly, it hurt because it broke my Mae's heart."

There were no words that would make that past hurt any better. Would he be less angry if I told him my heart had broken too? Would that even make a difference? I tried to tell him when I first arrived over a month ago.

"Then, our Patrick killed himself, and the pain blossomed again," he said before turning out onto the street. I matched his strides. "He was thousands of miles from home and people who loved him. I hope you are not surprised to hear that your mother never really loved him."

I shook my head. I had learned that tidbit long before my father died. If I didn't want to believe it back then, her actions toward me over the years proved it. She constantly berated me for being so much like him, as if I had any control over my genetics. She had loved Diane because Diane could control me in a way she never could control my father. He was smart enough to walk away. I wouldn't be surprised, though I can't say for sure, if she had driven him to end it all using me as her weapon. Hell, she had used me for every other thing in her life. Still, I couldn't bring myself to hate my mother, even though I couldn't put anything past her either.

"So, when you showed up last month, after having rejected us all these years, I took all of my anger and pain out on you. Not intentionally, you see. I wasn't trying to hurt you, Jackson. I wasn't. I just wanted to test your intentions before I let you hurt Mae." He ran his fingers through his thinning white hair before he stopped and turned to look at me. "You were doing so well, and then that damn California girl showed up at the farm office, all high heels and arrogance. She reminded me so much of your mother that I lost track of what was right. I sent her down there to you hoping she was telling the truth, and you would be gone before you hurt us all again. I was surprised and confused when you sent her away."

He fell silent for a few moments, and I was suddenly taken aback by how much he had seemed to age in the last month, hell, in the past few moments. It was as if his anger and pain had sustained him all these years, and talking through them released him to be who he was now.

"What changed your mind? I won't say that I'm not both surprised and confused that you are here talking to me."

"Carol," he said plainly. "She came up the mountain on Thursday. She was in the house drinking tea with Mae when I got back from the farm. She told us about the type of man you are and how you had won her heart. She invited us to come here and see for ourselves. Mae wasn't taking no for an answer."

"Carol went up the mountain on Thursday?" It was more

of a rhetorical question, as I recalled our argument about her out-of-town delivery that day, but he nodded in response anyway.

"I walked her out, and before she left, she let me have it. Told me I'd been unfair to you since you arrived, that I had neglected the team, and put her and Clarissa in danger with that Freddy kid. She told me I was selfish and vindictive, and that she was disappointed to learn that about me. Yep, she really gave me what for." He chuckled before looking me straight in the eye. "Do right by her, boy. You've got a good one there. Please don't break her heart when you leave."

He started walking back toward the house without looking to see if I would follow. He still trusted that I'd be right behind him, but I was glued to that spot. She had gone up there to defend me to my grandparents. Tears burned the backs of my eyes, as my heart swelled. If I didn't already love that woman, I'd have fallen head over heels tonight. What an amazing Christmas this was turning out to be.

Nick was halfway up the driveway again when he turned to look for me. I was already running that way, and I passed him by on my way to the door.

"I'm not going anywhere, old man. I will spend the rest of my life making her as happy as I am in this moment."

I entered the house and found the living room empty. Voices came from behind the swinging kitchen door, and I burst through, scanning the room for Carol.

"Jackson, are you alright," my grandmother asked, concern in her eyes.

"I'm better than alright. I am the happiest I have been in forever, and I owe it all to this woman here." I said, grabbing Carol from where she was bent over in front of the oven, and swinging her around.

"What are you doing, silly man? Dinner is almost ready."

"What am I doing? Loving you, if you'll let me. And, if

you'll let me, I will spend the rest of our lives trying to make you as happy as you've made me."

A slow smile spread across her face. "Ok. Yes. I'll take you up on that promise."

I pulled her close for a kiss. From the corner of my eye, I saw Nick grab my grandmother's hand and kiss it. All was right in the world, and tomorrow would be a new beginning.

Bonus Scenes

FROM CLARISSA CHARMS THE WALLFLOWER

I'd never been up the mountain before. Truth be told, I'd hardly ever left Ardor Point since I was a kid, and we'd go on family vacations. As an adult, though, I'd stuck close to home, close to Carol and the floral shop where I felt accepted and safe. Though Carol sometimes questioned my choices, she never judged me for them or held them against me. She didn't make me second guess myself. I'd always been free to be creative in every sense of the word. That's really all I ever wanted. So when Carol invited me to visit the Branches mountain home, I was a little unsure. I'd never met Nick's wife before, and Nick sometimes looked at me like an oddity.

"Marc will be there," Carol said when she saw the uncertainty on my face.

"He hadn't mentioned it," I retorted.

Not that Marc told me everything he did every day of the

week, but we talked often enough that he probably would've mentioned going to Sunday dinner with Nick. I knew he was excited to have been asked to stay on at the tree farm in the off season. He really loved the forest and the mountain. He also liked working with Jackson. When Jackson had reconciled with his grandfather and decided not to return to California, Marc jumped at the chance to join their team full time. I'm not sure how happy his parents were about him not returning to school, but I'm glad he stayed close, even if I didn't get to see him as often as I had when he was at the pop-up shop before the holidays.

"Just because he didn't tell you doesn't make it any less true. What's up with you two anyway? You were inseparable a couple weeks ago."

I bristled at her insinuation that there was trouble in our relationship. "We both have to work, and it's not like we live in the same town."

She gave me a sideways glance, and my hackles rose more. She didn't let me in on the ins and outs of her relationship with Jackson, even though we all had to live through their ups and downs for the first month or so. That was more drama than I'd ever witnessed with Carol, and still she didn't want to talk about it. I also didn't want to admit how much I wanted to see Marc. I missed him. Having our late-night talks over the phone a couple times a week was not the same. I gave her a big sigh before agreeing. I had to play it off, else she wouldn't let the curiosity go.

"Oh good! I didn't want to have to make the drive up myself. Jackson will already be there, and I didn't want to close the shop for the whole day."

"Yeah. Yeah. I already said I'd go. You don't have to tell me you'd have rather made the trip with your boyfriend."

I caught her eyeroll and laughed. "Speaking of boyfriend, is he all moved in?" I asked, wanting to keep the attention on her.

"He still has to go back to California for the rest of his stuff, but I think he's procrastinating. I can't say I blame him."

"Really? Why?" As lovey dovey as the two of them had been these past couple weeks, I couldn't imagine he'd procrastinate making this move officially permanent.

She shook her head. "It's not my place to tell his story, but let's just say he'll have to deal with Diane and his mother when he goes. His mom is a narcissist, and, well, you've met Diane."

I shuddered at the mention of that woman. She was a real piece of work and gave me bad vibes from the moment she walked into their hotel. I was actually surprised that Jackson would have been with a woman like her. Finding out that his mom was a narcissist explained it some, though. I knew all about living with a narcissist and how hard it was not to get caught up choosing those same traits in others. Everything I'd done since I was a teen was to try and break the cycle, or rather to keep myself from falling into the patterns my mother had set for me. No one should have to deal with that.

"Why don't you go with him?"

"What?"

"Why don't you go and protect him from them? You handled Diane beautifully, and from what I heard, you did a great job telling old man Nick about himself."

She fell silent, and I could tell she was mulling over my suggestion. I was surprised she hadn't already considered the idea herself. It seemed like the perfect solution. He shouldn't have to deal with that alone, and she wouldn't be here worried about him, making me crazy in the process. At least, that was the logic Marc had used on me when he volunteered to attend Christmas morning with my family. Though my mom had been on her best behavior when he came through the first time a week earlier, she totally went on a rant about him, my choices of friends, well, really all my life choices. I considered skipping out on the holidays altogether because of it until he offered to be my buffer. I hadn't explained all the details to

Carol, so she assumed mom had invited Marc as my boyfriend. *If only.*

"Welcome back, boss lady!" I yelled through the floral shop.

I had no idea where Carol was, but her car in the parking lot told me she was here. Jackson took her on an actual vacation to the Caribbean, and I couldn't wait to hear all about it. She came pushing through the swinging door of the workroom with a basket of clipped flowers in her hands.

"There you are," she said, as if I were late.

I'd not been late in the eleven years I'd worked for her. In fact, I'd been on time more often than she had these past few month, ever since Jackson moved in. Of course, I don't care that she's been late because this is the happiest I've seen her in all that time.

"Just because you showed up on time this morning," I said with a raised brow.

"It helps to be well-rested," she retorted.

"You're trying to tell me Jackson didn't spend the whole week blowing that back out?"

She cut her eyes at me, and I roared with laughter. Though she was not innocent at all, and neither was I, she always tried to pretend I shocked her with my innuendo. Okay, maybe I did manage to shock her occasionally. When she told me about the sexual escapades of young Carol, she didn't mention sexual talk or jokes. So maybe. At any rate, she should've been used to me by now. As soon as she put the flowers on the counter, I grabbed her in a tight hug. I had missed her, and not just because I had to run this place all by myself.

"I missed you too, Rissa." She laughed and turned to hug me back.

"So, what did you bring me?" I crossed my arms and tapped my foot.

She laughed again and went back to arranging the flowers on the counter. "How is it that I finally take a vacation after all these years, but you get a gift?"

I maintained my stance. "Because you love me. Because you missed me. Because this place didn't burn to the ground. Shall I go on?" I tilted my head to the other side.

Without lifting her eyes from the flowers, she tipped her head toward the workroom. A smile broke across my face, and I clapped like a kid before rushing through the swinging door. I didn't notice anything out of the ordinary at first and almost turned back around until I saw the box laid across the large worktable. It was so large, I mistook it for the tabletop at first.

"This huge box in here?" I yelled back to the shop.

Rather than answer, Carol came through the door, her face deadpanned. I stared at her quizzically until the corner of her mouth lifted. I took a tentative step toward the box. It was approximately six foot long by four foot wide and two foot deep. What in the world could she have possibly brought me back from the islands in a box like this. There's no way this fit on the plane.

"You didn't bring this back from your trip," I said firmly.

"Oh, but I did. I was on vacation, and I brought this with me today when I returned. Therefore, I brought it back from my trip. Just maybe not the trip you thought."

My eyes went wide, and my brain started playing through all the possibilities. "Did you guys change your mind about the all-inclusive resort?"

She chuckled. "Not at all. We had a great time."

"Then..."

She cut me off. "Just open it, Rissa. It's as much a gift as a proposition."

That statement confused me even more. What kind of proposition was she making?

"Stop overthinking and open it before we get customers."

I looked back at her, but she stood in the same spot, her face firmly set. She would not give me a clue. Grabbing a box cutter from a stand to my right, I cut the tape holding the flaps closed. It was taped so well, I had to cut around each side and across the top. Whoever packaged this did not want it coming open. Carol still hadn't moved other than to lean against the doorjamb. I pulled each of the four flaps open to reveal a huge slab of styrofoam the same dimensions as the box. When my brows drew in, a small giggle came from across the room, making me purse my lips.

"You're really enjoying this, aren't you?"

She shrugged but said nothing, so I gave my attention back to the box. Lifting the styrofoam, I gasped and my knees turned to jelly. I held the slab so tightly that I heard it crack and with it my control. Tears ran down my cheeks. This couldn't be for real. I pulled the styrofoam off completely and dropped it to the floor, taking in the full view. I ran my hand over the sign before me. This couldn't be real. I looked toward Carol through the tears. She was standing across the table from me watching my face closely.

"Are you for real?" I asked, my voice choked.

"I have a plan for the future," Carol said. "Jackson and I spent a good deal of our time talking about options for our future. I can't imagine you not being in it, but I can't just expect you to stay on as my assistant forever. I want to buy a small farm to grow my own flowers, and I want you to have a place to show your art. I'm hoping we can combine the two into a single creative vision."

She stepped around the table toward me, and I was frozen in shock.

"You are like a sister to me and the closest thing I will ever have to a kid of my own. I would be honored if you'd be my business partner."

"I...I...I" I swallow and take a deep breath. "I don't know what to say, C. Are you serious?"

"It's a yes or no question, Rissa. But please don't make me send this huge ass sign back."

The pleading look on her face made me giggle. I looked back down at the beautiful sign with flowers and paintbrushes around the new name, C & C Galleries.

"What does Jackson think about this?"

"This has nothing to do with him. It was you and me before anyone else stepped foot in this shop. If you say yes, it'll be you and me here until the end."

My lips pull up at the corners. That is the Carol I know and love. Spunky, protective, and loyal. She will never know how much I look up to and need her in my life.

"Let's do this thing."

"Thank goodness. Damn, you had me holding my breath!"

"It's called edging. Ask Jackson about it," I said with a wink and hugged her tightly, not even waiting to see her turn red.

About the Author

Leya Layne is a new author who has spent her entire life reading prolifically. Romance became one of her first loves, when, as a teen, she discovered a bag of Harlequin Romances beneath her grandmother's dresser. This holiday story was her first published novel, and holds a special place in her heart. That is why it deserved a rerelease. Hopefully, you enjoy the additions and look forward to reading Clarissa and Marc's story coming for Valentine's Day 2025.

Follow Leya all over social media:
https://linktr.ee/LeyaLayneAuthor

Other Leya Layne Novels:

You've Got Bookmail
Shar's Story

Coming in September 2024:
A limited-release, Cozy Fall Romance Anthology called Falling
in Cole County

Made in the USA
Columbia, SC
19 August 2024

40239246R00105